The Dream Planet of
Galloway

M E L Busst

authorHOUSE®

AuthorHouse™ UK
1663 Liberty Drive
Bloomington, IN 47403 USA
www.authorhouse.co.uk
Phone: 0800.197.4150

Published by AuthorHouse   11/27/2014

ISBN: 978-1-4969-9738-8 (sc)
ISBN: 978-1-4969-9739-5 (e)

This book is dedicated with love and affection to my dear nan Lily, who would have loved to have seen my first book published, and to my loyal dog Oscar, who never failed to inspire me.

CHAPTER ONE

The Royal Westneck

It all started with a smaller planet than ours – not terribly far from Earth, but no one could see it. It drifts through our galaxy and around our sun, as small as a piece of dust. The planet is called Galloway, the place where our dreams go. The energy from our dreams flows there, travelling in a mist of glittery dust which makes the planet grow and come to life. With water, land, trees and plants, and a haze of clouds drifting through its atmosphere, the planet seems just like ours … but is it?

On the planet of Galloway, drifting through the darkness in its open waters, with candlelight glowing from lanterns on its masts and wind blowing through its sails, there was a tall wooden ship. The *Royal Westneck* rode the waves of the Iffic Ocean with ease. A small young man scrubbed the deck on his hands and knees, his white shirt covered in grime, blending him into the darkness, though the silver belt buckle of his worn black trousers caught the candlelight. His long blonde hair bobbed as he scrubbed the deck as hard as he could, sweat pouring down his face.

"Hills!" someone shouted behind him.

"Hills! C'mon!" A tall, slim figure appeared wearing a blue hat and navy blue coat. A yellow stripe ran down his right side, indicating his rank. He paused behind Hills, who continued scrubbing.

"*Hills!*" he shouted, jabbing the youth in the back.

"Yes!" Hills jumped. "I'm sorry, sir; I was in my own world, sir."

"Kimy Hills, it's me. I'm not an officer: I'm a sergeant, and you will call me Sergeant Peng! C'mon, boy, it's time to stop. You smell of sweat and you're drenched!"

Peng helped Kimy to his feet and walked with him to the stairs that lead to the decks below.

"How long has it been?" asked Kimy, leaning on the banister as he struggled to walk.

"Too long." Peng guided him down a step at a time. Kimy made it to his hammock, which gracefully swung from side to side. He finally managed to lie down, using Peng for support and steadying his moving bed.

"Thank you, Sergeant."

He rested his head gently on his green pillow and closed his eyes. Peng stood by and looked down at Kimy's face for a moment. He touched his own, running his finger along a large scar on his left cheek and sighed before walking away.

Where Kimy slept was dirty and dark. Only two or three lamps perched on wooden pillars lined the walkway. Hammocks were on every side, swaying in time with the ship. Beneath the hammocks lay the weapons. Their black coats rested on wooden platforms, and carefully stacked cannon balls patiently waited by their sides to load the ship's twenty-four guns. On the starboard side of the deck stood an old wooden table covered in crumbs and wine stains. Many a drunken sailor had knocked his brew off the side and slumped to sleep on its top or had stood up too quickly in order to deliver a blow after losing a game of cards. The table could have told a few tales. At the end of the lower deck was a tall cupboard filled with machetes, pistols, and knives. These arms had seen battle with many other ships.

The door beside the cupboard swung open, and a man emerged from the darkness, grinning. A bright blue feather took pride of place in his hat. A golden brown pattern ran around the brim. The man's flushed face contrasted oddly with his grey unkempt beard. His green-and-white cotton shirt was full of holes and revealed his enormous stomach, which protruded between the missing buttons. He walked with a slight limp, his left hand clenching into a fist as he approached Kimy's hammock, stopping at his feet for only a second before sharply grabbing the ropes that held it to the ceiling.

"Take this!" he laughed while swinging Kimy's hammock violently.

"Get off!" shouted Kimy as he held on tight to the edges, desperately trying not to fall out. "Stop it, you fat drunk!"

"Ooh, I didn't see you there, rat boy! Ha ha, look at you. You don't belong on this ship, Hills." He pressed his fat sweaty face close to him. "Now look here, boy. Your daddy is high up the ranks and trying to get you to follow in his footsteps." Kimy's eyes widened at the man's stench. "But you won't be good enough for his job because you're a weakling that cries at the sight of war."

"Poll, I don't give a damn if my father has the highest rank, but I *do* give a damn if you ever get there 'cause you will stink out the Council Hall with your smell!"

A thick hand grabbed Kimy's throat and squeezed. "You dare say that!" Kimy gasped for breath as a second hand followed the first. "One day ... one day soon ..." Poll shook Kimy, pulling him from his hammock. "I will be the best man of them all, and all the Hills family will kiss my feet, but no, instead I'm a cook for the *Royal Westneck* instead of the captain of the *Whitejack*."

"Poll, get off Hills!" shouted a voice from the entrance.

"Oh sorry, Sergeant, I didn't see him." Poll quickly took his hands off Kimy's throat.

"Don't play stupid games with me!" Peng walked over to Kimy.

"Get up. The captain wants to see you."

"Whoopee-doo! Mr Weakling's gonna see Thin-sticks," said Poll.

"Shut up, Poll, you ungrateful maggot!" shouted the sergeant as he and Kimy walked out onto the upper deck.

The captain was indeed a thin fellow with thin black hair, a narrow face, and a mole in the middle of his right cheek. His red boots gleamed and his neatly ironed grey trousers boasted crisp creases, though they weren't apparent as he sat at his desk in his quarters.

"Now look here, Kimy," advised the sergeant as the two walked towards the quarters, "Captain Glabeo is a dark man. Whatever you do, don't disappoint him."

"What does he want me for?" asked Kimy.

"I don't know, but he worked with your father while fighting in the Battle of Cans," said the sergeant as he knocked on the door with three taps.

"Kimy, don't take Poll to heart. He's just a drunk."

"'Course not," replied Kimy as he entered the room.

"Kimy Hills," said Captain Glabeo, tapping the desk with the palm of his hand, his boots propped up on his desk. He glanced up from some papers to say, "I worked with your father, you know. What a great man he is. Come and sit down."

"Thank you, sir," said Kimy as he approached the captain's desk.

"Kimy, I want to know why I found you on a small boat out in the middle of nowhere."

"Yes, sir. I was lost from my ship, the *Fortune*."

"I don't think so …" said Glabeo as he got up. "I think you are running from something, but I don't know what." He started to pace behind his desk, his hands held behind his back and thumbs twitching. "Tell me, Kimy, what's the secret?"

"There's no secret, sir. I was sent on a training mission. They sent four of us out in lifeboats to search the surrounding area, but when we returned, the ship was gone, sir!" said Kimy, staring at the desk.

"Yet I found only you on your own. Where are the others?"

"Well …" replied Kimy. "I don't know how to explain it …" His hands twisted together in his lap.

"C'mon, Kimy, is it that bad?"

"They were there, sir, and then they were gone."

"You mean to say they just vanished into thin air? Come on, that's not possible!"

"I know, sir, but that's the truth!" pleaded Kimy with a hint of panic in his voice. He could see anger lurking in the captain's face.

"I'm fed up with this. Every time I ask you, it's just the same old story!" shouted Glabeo. He approached the window and stared out at the ocean as it twinkled under the night's sky. It appeared to calm him slightly. "Kimy, having worked with your father, I know that he believes you to be the best seaman ever to sail in these waters, but right now I don't believe it."

"But, sir, I'm telling the truth! I'm not lying!" Kimy stood, his eyes fixed on the captain. Glabeo turned to face him and snapped his fingers, and in an instant two men entered and stood behind Kimy's chair.

"Take Hills to the chamber in the storage deck," Glabeo demanded as he returned to his desk. Kimy looked surprised and stared directly into his captain's eyes as the men took him by either arm and dragged him out the door.

"*I'm telling the truth!*" shouted Kimy at the top of his lungs, but Glabeo ignored him. "Please, sir, *no!*" he shouted as he disappeared down the stairs.

One of the men laughed. "The captain hates you, don't he? Maybe he'll find a nice little island to stick you on." the two wrestled Kimy along a dark, damp corridor.

"Let me go!" Kimy made his final attempt to free himself from their grips.

"Hey!" one of the men shouted as Kimy pulled them down to the ground, having lunged backwards with his fists, smacking them both in the mouth. All three toppled backwards, making a loud thump as they hit the deck.

"Get him!" one shouted as Kimy jumped up and ran back down the corridor. He reached the door at the end, but the men were already scrambling up behind him, their guns out. They fired shot after shot, narrowly missing Kimy's shoulders and taking chunks out of the wood. Kimy leapt and crashed through the door, shattering the frame as he fell to the galley. The two men rushed in and pinned him to the ground. One held him down as the other handcuffed him.

"That's it, Hills, you're going down!" one shouted as Kimy once again tried to free himself from their grip. They dragged Kimy by his handcuffs to the other end of the corridor, and the one with a black curly beard reached into his back pocket and pulled out a large set of keys.

"Ah, here it is," he sighed.

Kimy began to struggle once more, but a wave of pain put a stop to that as he was punched hard in the stomach. Kimy curled up in agony on the floor where the men dropped him.

"Ah, we seem to have found a killer," the man without the keys said as he grabbed Kimy's chin. The other man unlocked the door to the dark, stinking storage room, and they threw Kimy backwards into a cage.

"Oh yes, you're our boy now." They slammed the cage door, and Kimy just lay there, covering his head with his cuffed hands.

"You won't last a week with us," one said, and they walked out of the room laughing. They slammed the door behind them, which plunged Kimy into complete darkness. All he could hear was the sound of water dripping into a bucket. He turned around and sat up, holding his knees tightly as he tried to make out the place, slowly his eyes adjusted to the darkness. All he could see were weird outlines of different objects, some round, others square. Then something caught Kimy's eye as it skirted under another object and then reappeared, racing along the floor and out of Kimy's vision though he could still hear it – the sound of claws running along the wooden floor. Kimy put his head down. He wondered what he had done wrong to get himself into this, but then he heard something else and crawled to the other side of the cage. He listened carefully to the sound of footsteps coming from above and then the sound of music arose, along with the echoes of laughter.

"This is great!" one of them shouted.

"Yes, it's my favourite piece," another replied with a posh accent.

"Would you like a dance?"

"Yes, of course."

Then a loud thud shot through the ceiling, and another, and another, all night long until Kimy fell asleep.

CHAPTER TWO

The House of Stone

As an ordinary day dawned in the port of the capital city, Gollo, tall ships arrived with different kinds of cargo, and residents saw nothing unusual. However, in the centre of the city, in a building made of the finest stone, it was a different scene entirely. The House of Stone, as the Council Hall was sometimes called, was filled with shouting, fighting, and arguing.

"I'm sick of this! One of the defence ministers must take responsibility for the control of defence of our ships."

"Yes, I agree. Going into the Dark Sea was the wrong thing to do!" shouted Carrot, the man who owned the golden trade of cargo ships, otherwise known as the Golden Fleet.

"I understand, Carrot, but it will cost more doubloons to sail through the Coconut Sea than to go through the Dark Sea," said Minister William Seamore. His long black coat billowed as he sat down.

"The Royal Sails cannot defend your ships from counterattacks. We have too much to lose," added Foofur Hills, who was the Royal Sails Minister and Kimy's father. He had blue curly hair and a blue moustache that flicked up at either end. Foofur Hills was a very tall man, and today he wore a grand red robe with gold stitching that seemed to emphasise his height, and a black-and-red leather hat with lace that hung down at the back.

"So, what are we going to do about it? My trade ships are out there, disappearing in numbers," Carrot acknowledged, his black hat covering his red hair and long black coat skimming the ground. "And the cargo! It's as though these ships are faster than mine," he grumbled and glanced at the only man there who wore a crown with his red-and-gold patterned robes. "King John, what are we going to do?"

"We can't extend our defence of the Golden Fleet because we don't have enough to guard Gollo from an invasion as it is. We lost a third of our fleet in May, fighting against pirates." King John stood up and brushed his silky long brown hair behind him.

Suddenly the massive wooden doors at the back of the hall swung open as a small man rushed in, muttering to himself under his hooded black robes. He hurried to the centre of the room, where the long table always stood, and slammed a pile of books onto it.

"Who is this?" shouted King John in astonishment. The hooded man ignored him and just stood there, muttering under his breath and tugging at his tattered clothes in distraction.

"Hello! You there! What do you think you're doing?" This time the king pointed at the man.

"My name is Peter Cake, Your Majesty. I am an inventor, and I have come up with a great bit of work which will make travelling much faster than a horse and cart!" He flicked through the pages of one of his books and stopped roughly in the middle. "Look here, Your Majesty." He ran up towards the king and placed the book upon his lap.

"What am I looking at?" asked King John.

"Well, you are looking at a carriage that runs by steam power – without a horse in sight!" proclaimed Mr Cake.

"How does it work?"

"This is the good part. I call it an 'engine'. It's made of metal, with steel piping and with pistons that move up and down. Steam is produced by water, heated from burning coal, and is then sent through the engine to make the wheels turn! If you don't believe me, then come outside and look!"

"This is just rubbish," Carrot grumbled, placing his head in his hands. "My ships are falling in numbers, and you let this wacko inventor charge in here and change the subject. Your Majesty, may we return to the topic at hand?" Carrot's impatience was clearly growing.

"Hmmm," said King John as he looked at Peter Cake's invention.

"You say this can run without a horse, and faster?"

"Yes, I do," replied Peter.

"How can you steer this contraption?"

"By using two wooden sticks which sit between your legs. When you pull the one on the right, it turns right and vice versa." The inventor pointed at the drawing in his book as he spoke.

The king paused for a minute. "Well, yes… could you make an engine for a ship?"

"I don't know. It's a big thing to do. I'm not sure it will work for a ship, Your Majesty." Peter replied as he walked back towards the large wooden table.

"This is important, and I want you to do it," demanded the king.

"But, Your Majesty—"

"No buts. That is an order. If you can make an engine for a cart, then you can make one for a ship." The king stood up. "Foofur Hills, let Mr Cake use one of your shipyards. This ship will be the fastest in the sea!"

"King John, we need the shipyards in order to build a fleet to defend us!" Foofur pointed out furiously.

"I will not repeat myself," the king replied sternly.

"Your Majesty, what about my ships?" Carrot added.

"Foofur, is there a ship near the Dark Sea?" asked the king.

"Only the *Royal Westneck* is out there."

"Let the *Royal Westneck* guard the Golden Fleet then."

"But, Your Majesty—"

"Do it!" shouted King John.

Foofur Hills walked out of the hall and into the packed lobby, where he bumped into a short, chubby man wearing his royal uniform.

"Ah, Major Waddle, how are you?" asked Foofur.

"I'm all right. How's the meeting going?"

"We've got to get the *Royal Westneck* to guard the Golden Fleet."

"Is the king mad?"

"I don't know. I told him we have no defence, but he wouldn't listen!"

"Well, it is down to the king if we get invaded by pirates."

They walked together slowly out the front door, down the stony steps, and onto the dusty road.

"I've asked James and his fiancée over for tea this evening. Would you care to join us?" Foofur asked.

"Yes, that would be lovely. Is Rosetta cooking her famous roast rabbit with green slug?"

"Oh yes!"

"Great, I'll be there!" Waddle climbed into a carriage at the side of the road.

"Oh, hold on, there's one more thing".

"What?"

"There was an inventor named Peter Cake. He has apparently created a cart that runs by a thing he calls an engine instead of a horse."

"Is the man dreaming?" Waddle laughed as he slammed the carriage door shut.

"The king has asked him to build one for a ship, using one of our yards," added Foofur.

"Great!" Waddle shouted sarcastically through the open window as the carriage pulled away.

Chapter Three

Green Tree Palm

Foofur walked up a steep bending road leading out of the city and down a country lane to where his cottage stood. Grey smoke puffed out of the chimney. The surroundings were beautiful and quiet. The area was called Green Tree Palm after the trees nearby. Fields of vibrant green sat on either side of the lane, and the sound of singing birds and horses neighing made Foofur feel immediately at peace as he walked up to his home. As he opened the door, he inhaled deeply.

"Rosetta, that is the best smell to come home to after a hard day," he said as he stepped into the lounge, where he saw the fire blazing.

"Hello, dear!" said a voice coming from the kitchen.

Foofur smiled at the sweet tone and entered the kitchen, where he saw his beautiful wife in a white silk dress with her long blonde hair down. It looked so soft that Foofur could not stop himself from running his fingers through it as he embraced her in greeting.

"Did you have a good day, dear?" Rosetta asked as she made her way towards the oven and looked inside.

"No, not really," Foofur replied as he looked into the fruit bowl deciding which piece to take. "The king wants us to send the *Royal Westneck* to the Golden Fleet in the middle of the Dark Sea." He pinched off a few grapes.

"Oh dear. In the newspapers they think the ships are being sucked under by a powerful force," said Rosetta as she stirred the simmering pot of greens.

"It's utterly ridiculous, anyway how was your day, darling?" Foofur asked.

"It's been okay. I didn't sell much at the market – just my orange soup with greens."

"I've got to go to Finley in the morning for a few days."

"Not again! You are never home; you're always away."

"I'm sorry, but something has come up."

"I hope you will be home for Christmas, as last year you weren't."

"I promise to be here for Christmas," Foofur said as he sat down at the table.

"And what of Kimy?" Rosetta struggled to get the words out.

Foofur looked grim. "That's why I didn't want the *Royal Westneck* going to guard the fleet. I want it to look for the ship that our son was on."

Rosetta started crying as she took the rabbit out of the oven.

"I wish that he had never joined the Royal Sails. I wish that he was home with me. You know he didn't want to go, but you had to insist."

"It's for his own good."

"No, it isn't. It's just your family tradition," cried Rosetta as she put the spuds in the oven.

"Every member of my family has to do it. There's no other option."

"Yes, there is, Foofur – an option that you could have gave him, but you wanted him to follow in your footsteps as the Royal Sails Minister."

"That's not true. I only wanted him to do well for himself," Foofur argued as Rosetta leaned over the worktop to look longingly out the window.

"Ah great! James and Puss are here!" she said as she waved through the window. "Why are you stricter with Kimy than you are with James?"

"Kimy is more skittish and lacks direction, but he is a good sailor."

"But don't you think you are pushing him too hard to go your way?"

"No, I don't. I am helping him, and sometimes I have to be strict with him."

"But what about James? You are kinder to him, and you spend more time with him than Kimy. What if Kimy is dead? What then?" Rosetta said as she burst into tears once again. "It's been four weeks!" She wiped tears from her eyes.

The back door swung open. "Hello," boomed a deep voice as a young man with blue hair walked in with one hand full of flowers.

"It's so great to see you, James," Rosetta said as she approached him and kissed him on the cheek.

"These are for you, Mum," James replied as he handed over the flowers.

"They are beautiful! Lemonera, my favourites."

"Hello, Rosetta, Foofur," said Puss as she followed James in. She wore a pretty flowery dress, and her black hair was neatly tied back in a bun, hiding the glimmer of red towards the ends that it often showed.

"How's dinner coming along, Mum? I'm starving!" James said as he sat down next to Foofur.

"It won't be long now."

"Rosetta, are you entering the soap competition?" Puss asked.

"Yes, of course I am, my dear. I always enter."

"Dad, how's the search going?" asked James.

"Not good, Son." Foofur sighed. "They want us to call it off."

"Why?"

"They want the *Royal Westneck* to guard the Golden Fleet from attack in the Dark Sea."

"And still no sign at all?" James pressed.

"No, not that I have heard."

A loud knock on the front door interrupted the conversation.

"Ah, Major Waddle is here," Foofur said and stood to answer the door.

"Are you okay?" Puss asked Rosetta as she filled the rabbit with slug.

"Yes, dear, of course."

"C'mon, you're not okay!" Puss said as she put her arms around her.

"My son is out there, on his own!" wailed Rosetta as she tried to fill the rabbit.

"I'm sure that Kimy is okay."

"I hope so."

"He's a fighter, Rosetta; he will be back."

"I don't know, darling. I hope for the best – that he can find his way home."

Major Waddle made his way through the door, his wooden leg creaking with each step he took across the kitchen floor.

"Hello, Major Waddle," Rosetta said.

"How is my lovely girl keeping?" Major Waddle sat at the table, careful not to trip on his coat.

"I'm great, sir, but still missing Kimy." Rosetta placed the stuffed rabbit back in the oven.

"I'm sure he is fine, Mrs Hills. Your son is strong! Of course he will be back. He misses your lovely cooking!"

"Yes, Kim does love my cooking, especially my coco-chicken. That's his favourite."

"The thing is, Major," said James, "our planet expands every year, and you know it will grow again at New Year when the Gates of Dreams open. If Kimy is out there still, it could be very dangerous if he is near one of the gates."

"If Kimy is at one of the four gates of Galloway, yes," agreed the major. "But I think he would know better than to be out at that time. Anyway the gates are only open for an hour."

"I just hope they find my brother before it happens," James said, and no one could argue with that.

CHAPTER FOUR

A Surprise from the Sky

After dinner, while everyone was waiting for some tea to brew, James picked up the newspaper and he saw an odd picture. It was a fleet of ships at night, lit only by lanterns and lightning, but in the corner, he could just make out something like a tentacle coming from the sea. The article accompanying the picture said a great pirate ship of ghosts was attacking the Golden Fleet for the treasures that the ships were carrying. They were called ghosts because they always attacked in the dark, snuffing out even their smallest candles. However, others were saying that it wasn't pirates at all – that there was a greater force sucking the ships under water. The next article said that another ship had been attacked by pirates from the Mullet Islands during the night as the crew were asleep in their bunks. James started thinking that the two incidents were related, but how? He stared at the picture, deep in thought.

"This was not done by pirates," he finally said out loud as Rosetta put his tea in front of him.

"What do you mean?"

"Look, there's something here" James showed her the picture.

"I can't see anything, James; it just looks like a fleet at night."

"There is, I know there is," James insisted, half to himself.

"I think this *thing* did the same to the ship Kimy was on."

"I don't think so, James," Foofur interrupted. "How can it be the same thing if it's not pirates, when the two ships were many miles away? It's just pirates in the dark that's all."

"I don't think so. I've got a feeling that there will be worse things happening out there, and Kimy is in the middle of it all."

"Oh, no!" cried Rosetta.

"Stop it, James, you're making your mother cry," Foofur said sternly. "Let's have our tea."

As the evening wore on, James kept wondering about the creature in the newspaper. The thought of his brother being out there with it made him shiver.

"James," said Major Waddle as he tapped him on the shoulder.

James jumped.

"I'm sorry, James, I didn't mean to startle you."

"Not at all, Major. I was thinking of Kimy again."

"Oh, James, don't worry about Kimy. He will be fine."

"How do you know?" asked James harshly. "All you people think about is money. It makes me sick!"

"James, calm down. I know how you are feeling," said Foofur.

"No you don't, Dad. My little brother is out there on his own, probably with no food or water," argued James, "and all you lot are worried about is the Golden Fleet." James stood up. "I'm more worried about my brother than that fleet of old ships!"

"I'm worrying about him too, James, but the king is more worried about the Golden Fleet than Kimy."

James stalked away. "Puss, go and see if he's all right," Rosetta said as she collected all the dirty cups.

James was found at the back of the lounge, next to the bookshelf, looking into the glass of gin he had just poured.

"James, come on, a drink is not going to help," said Puss as she sat on the yellow couch beside him, taking his glass out of his hand and setting it on the coffee table. "I know you're worried about Kim, and I know you want to go out there to find him, but taking it out on your father is not the right thing to do." She gently took his hand.

"Don't I know that," replied James. "I only wish that Kim was at home right now."

Out the back of the cottage was a wooden shed that looked over Rosetta's fish pond. Gentle light poured out of the window as Rosetta pointed Major Waddle to the bags of oranges he had offered to carry in for her.

"Wow," said Major Waddle, "your oranges are big, Mrs Hills. And these are the ones from your own trees?"

"Yes, of course they are."

"How do you do it?" asked Major Waddle.

"That's my secret," she answered with a smile as they walked back towards the cottage. But, as they approached the door, a weird feeling came over Major Waddle, as though something were watching him. He turned around, drawing his pistol as he did, scanning the area.

"What is it, Major?" asked Rosetta, looking scared.

"I don't know, my dear; just get back to the cottage. Something smells funny." Waddle stood there, staring towards the garden, with the wind whistling through the trees. Rosetta walked slowly backwards into the enclosed porch, where she knelt down, looking out the window to check on Major Waddle. Suddenly a beam of light flashed down to the back of the garden from the sky above, setting the trees and bushes below on fire. White smoke flowed out of the garden, obscuring Rosetta's vision. She couldn't see Major Waddle anymore. As she opened the door, a great wall of hot air hit her.

"Major Waddle, Major Waddle!" she shouted but got no reply. All she could hear was the crackling sound that came from the fire. The heat was unbearable as she walked slowly back out into the garden, shouting for Major Waddle. Then a great roar shook the ground, making Rosetta fall over and roll down the steps.

Major Waddle walked through the woodland with his pistol held high, trying to peer through the misty smoke that surrounded the area. He walked swiftly from tree to tree, grabbing onto a trunk each time the creature roared. As Major Waddle came upon a great oak tree, he saw the fire at a distance, eating up the farthest edge of the woodland. Major Waddle knelt down behind the oak, looking at the puffs of fire coming up out of the undergrowth. He stared, trying to see the creature as a long black tail knocked over bits of wood, making the ground tremble as it burrowed underground, sending up fire as it went. Major Waddle stayed still, his eyes looking on in despair as parts of the ground heaved up as the creature dug its way through. Trees toppled as streams of fire shot up out of the cracks in the soil.

James and Foofur rushed out of the cottage door and hid behind the stone wall. "Look James!" shouted Foofur as he loaded his gun. "I want you to stay here and cover my back."

"Why? I won't be able to see you," said James as he peered up over the wall, and saw the ground tremble dramatically.

"I'm going over to that blackberry bush, over there," said Foofur as he tried to hold onto the wall. "James, look!"

A great wave of fire shot up out of the woodland, blazing high.

"There's no time!" shouted Foofur as he rushed down to where it came from.

Waddle was now lying on the ground, looking through the gaps between the roots of the oak tree as a black creature appeared out of the smoke. Major Waddle pushed himself more into the ground as he watched it walk forward until it stopped by a tree.

"Oh dear." Major Waddle panicked as he pointed his gun at it, his hands trembling in fright. A bright red light shot out the black creature's eyes as it beamed through the woodland.

"Crikey!" cried Major Waddle, as it blasted past him, ripping the side of his coat, but as Major Waddle looked back the creature was gone. All he could see was the tree where it had been standing.

Foofur crawled through the blackberry bush, looking across the pond. Fire was raging around it as he crawled down the bank. A red blaze suddenly burst through the garden and smashed the windows of the cottage as it hit.

"Puss!" bellowed James as he hid behind the wall, glass shattering around him. He crawled along the side of the wall. A blast of fire burst through the broken windows, making James crawl faster to the door.

"Puss!" he shouted again and again. As he reached the door, a loud scream came from the lounge.

"Puss, I'm coming!" shouted James as he barged through the entrance, covering his mouth with his hand as he ran through the fire in the kitchen, which singed the bottom of his trousers. James tripped over a chair leg as he ran into the lounge and landed heavily on the floor beside the coffee table.

"Argh!" he yelled out in pain, his left leg on fire.

"Puss, where are you?" he shouted at the top of his lungs as he grabbed a pillow off the sofa and smothered the fire burning his leg.

Outside, Foofur rushed through the woodland as fast as he could to reach Major Waddle, who was looking down into a gigantic hole in the ground.

"My goodness," he said as he stopped beside him.

"Something is terribly wrong," said Waddle, "for a bad dream to just crash on us like that. Something must have happened to the Gates of Dreams."

"These dreams are too powerful for the gates to hold," replied Foofur, as they gazed down the big black smoky hole.

CHAPTER FIVE

The Creature in Dark Waters

As the *Royal Westneck* sailed quietly into the Dark Sea, the only sound was of the ship creaking. Kimy lay on the cage floor, which smelt of rotting food. Suddenly, the door of the storage room burst open.

"Come on, wakey wakey!" shouted Sergeant Peng as he slapped his stick against the cage bars.

"Time to get up, Hills. You are needed on deck." Kimy just stared into space.

"Come on, Hills." Peng pulled him to his feet.

"Why did the captain do this to me?" asked Kimy, his eyes only half open.

"I don't know, Hills, but we need you up on deck." He pushed Kimy out the door.

Out on the deck, the crew stood in two rows, looking out into the dark blue sea. Glabeo stood at the end of the ship, looking down his long silver telescope.

"Here he is, sir," said Peng as he walked towards him with Kimy.

"Kimy," said Glabeo, "this is a good thing for you." He put down his telescope. "I know you are doing your captain's training. Let's see if we can put you to the test." Glabeo walked around the youth, putting his hands on Kimy's shoulders.

"What do you mean, Captain?" asked Kimy.

"Your father has sent us to guard the Golden Fleet, which has been attacked by a group of killers. I only hope that you can find these ships before they find us. I want you to stay all night and all day, through storm or rain, up there in the lookout until you spot them."

Glabeo handed Kimy the telescope.

"Oh yes, and they have their lanterns off," he said as he went to the ladder to go below. Kimy looked up at the tall main mast with giddiness. Kimy had been petrified of heights since falling from a tree back home when he was ten.

"Why me?" wondered Kimy as he and another youngster with rather tattered clothing got loaded onto the wooden lift. Kimy looked up at the lookout as they were heaved up.

"Don't be scared," said the young man as he ate a piece of bread while leaning on the side.

"I don't like heights."

"Hey, neither do I. My name's Rusty Miller." The small young man put out his hand.

"Oh, yes, I'm Kimy Hills." He said as he shook it.

"Come on." Rusty said as the lift reached the top. He climbed the rope to the lookout. Kimy looked up at him as he put out his hand. "Come on," he repeated.

Kimy was shaken up just from being in the lift. "I can't do this."

"Come on, get off!" shouted up one of the men holding the rope to the lift.

"Don't look down; look at me," said Rusty as it started raining. Kimy took a deep breath and went for it, grabbing Rusty's arm.

"That's it." Rusty helped pull him up, lifting him over by his shirt. The rain was pouring now.

"That's just great!" shouted Rusty banging his hand on his side. "We've got to live up here in this."

Kimy got up off the floor of the lookout. "I'm going to throw up." He put his head over the side, vomiting onto the deck far below.

"Hey!" shouted a passer-by, lifting his fist towards Kimy and Rusty.

"Sorry, but that's the sick deck!" Rusty laughed.

"I'll get you!" shouted the man as he wiped off the sick with his hands.

"Are you better now?" asked Rusty.

"A little, but still giddy."

"Ah, don't worry, you'll get used to it." Rusty opened the telescope and gazed out to sea.

"Anything?" asked Kimy.

"No, nothing. So, where are you from?"

"I'm from Gollo. I live in the capital," Kimy said, sounding a little steadier.

"I live in the capital too, but on the outskirts."

"I'm sick of being on this ship. The captain hates me. I've stayed all week in the storage room," Kimy griped as he looked at his shabby boots.

"Yeah, the storage room. I've been in there a couple of times. Captain Glabeo is a stubborn old man."

"So how did you end up in there?"

"Got done for robbing food from the galley," said Rusty as he pulled out a steak from his waistcoat and smiled.

"I see." Kimy laughed.

"Here, do you want a piece?" Rusty tore off a bit.

"Yes, please, I haven't eaten in days." Kimy gorged on the juicy steak.

Kimy and Rusty took turns on lookout. Food and water came up to them by the lift. Weeks went by with no sight of the Golden Fleet. Kimy was starting to lose faith as he peered through the telescope out into the darkness.

"Damn it."

"What, still no ships?" asked Rusty.

"This is great!" shouted Kimy lifting his hands high.

"Calm down, mate!" Rusty looked as Kimy pointed up at the shining stars. "Yes, they are beautiful. I look up at these every night when I'm at home, wondering what's out there."

"Earth is out there."

"What's Earth?" Rusty asked.

"Earth is the place where all the dreams come from."

"What do you mean?"

"Our planet is controlled by the dreams that people on Earth have."

"I still don't get it."

"Look, our planet grows on dreams; you and I probably came from a dream."

"Ah …" said Rusty, scratching his head with confusion. "That's stupid."

"No, it's true. Why do you think we have to stay inside after New Year?"

"Because the sky turns purple?" Rusty joked.

"No, it's because the gates open and allow the dreams to go through."

"Come on, Kim, do you really believe that?" Rusty burst out laughing, slapping Kimy on his back as he sat down. "Where are you getting this from?"

"From my father."

"Do you believe everything your father says?"

"My father is the Royal Sails Minister. He knows about it."

"What?" shouted Rusty. "You're the son of Foofur Hills, the man at the height of it all?"

"Yes," replied Kimy, staring over the edge of the lookout feeling the wind blowing through his hair.

"Don't he know you're on this ship?" Rusty demanded.

"No. I don't think Captain Glabeo has sent a message."

"No, I suppose he wouldn't."

"So, what does your father do?" asked Kimy.

"I don't know my father."

"Oh … I'm sorry."

"Ah, don't be." Rusty stood up, wringing his hands together. "My father was a drunken slob, supposedly – at least, that's what my mother says. He ran away when my mother told him she was pregnant." Rusty took the telescope from Kimy.

"Have you tried to get in contact with him?"

"No, my mother won't let me. She says I won't be welcome. He's a bad man. Anyway, you must have it hard, what with your father being the Sails Minister."

"You could say that. I never wanted to join the Royal Sails. I would rather be a gardener."

"I see … But your father wants you to follow him?"

"I suppose so, but I'm not like him."

"What's this?" Rusty had raised the telescope again out of habit, but now he held still.

"What's out there?"

"Take a look."

Kimy looked down the telescope and saw something glowing in the distance. Then the ship shook fiercely. Kimy and Rusty fell onto the lookout floor. They lay there as the ship was forced sideways, leaning to port.

"Hold on!" shouted Kimy as the ship leaned more and shouting came from the crew on the deck below. Then two great tentacles heaved up out of the water, splashing waves onto the deck and grabbing onto the hull.

"Man the guns!" bellowed Captain Glabeo, rushing around the deck, pulling his crew to their feet and almost throwing them down the hatch.

"Man the guns, you bunch of cowards!"

Then from behind him an enormous tentacle came crashing down, forcing Glabeo to take cover. "This is it!" The captain pulled out his sword and charged, finally lunging at the tentacle. A loud rumble came from under the ship as Glabeo's sword ran through it.

"This is how you do it, you amateurs!" Glabeo shouted as he turned around, holding his sword dripping with blood.

"You are all weak! If you want to survive, you must be as crazy as me!" Glabeo laughed. "Kimy!" He looked up at the two men still high above the crew. "Do you want us to die?"

"No, sir!"

"You two have got to pay attention to the surrounding area!"

"Captain, there's a fire over to the ship's starboard" shouted Rusty.

"Great work, Miller! Much better than Hills. Turn the ship starboard!" shouted Glabeo, lifting his sword. As the ship turned, two more tentacles quickly wrapped around the masts, pulling the ship over and snapping them.

"Come on!" Glabeo shouted to his crew, who started to panic. Rusty and Kimy were left to hang on for their dear lives as the lookout tower plunged into the dark water.

"Man your positions!" shouted Sergeant Peng as he ran to the nearest gun, slipping as the ship heaved portside again. Kimy opened his eyes as he sank deeper and deeper, caught in the current. He could see canon fire above and heard the creature's roar. But then two green-and-black tentacles raced up only inches away from Kimy, sucking him towards it in its wake. Up and up he went with the water forcing him, not certain whether he should try to resist. The creature's tentacles surged out of the water, pointing up at the dark clouded sky above. Rusty had managed to stay close to the surface, though waves frequently plunged him under as he tried to stay afloat.

"Kimy, where are you?" Rusty shouted with water gushing into his mouth. The tentacle went up and up; Kimy was dragged with it, his shirt caught on a barb. He looked down at the *Royal Westneck,* at the crew running around like ants with cannons firing on both sides of the ship. The tentacle finally came to a stop; Kimy started feeling giddy as he waited for it to collapse down onto the *Royal Westneck.* He could feel the cold breeze hitting his face, freezing his right cheek. His hands turned white as he tried to reach for his sword; then suddenly half of his shirt came unstuck. Kimy dropped down and came to an abrupt stop with only the bottom half of his shirt holding him on. He managed to pull out his sword.

"Aaaaaaarrrrrrrrrrrrrghh!" shouted Kimy as he swung it up into the air as the gigantic tentacle started to lunge. Kimy plunged his sword into it as it heaved forward. A great roar from under the sea blew up gigantic bubbles.

Rusty was still floating in the water, trying to swim out of the way as cannonballs leapt into the sea around him. The great tentacle unintentionally holding Kimy, plunged back into the sea with an almighty splash that swept over the entire ship, soaking the crew still on board.

Captain Glabeo looked out at the place where the tentacle went down.

"Great, sir! No more Kimy Hills," said Poll as he came to the captain's side.

"What do you mean?" Glabeo turned to look at him.

"Hills was on that thing."

"Then Kimy Hills is a hero!"

"What?" Poll spat.

"Yes!" shouted Glabeo as all the crew looked at him. "We will remember Kimy Hills as the man who took down the great beast!"

Glabeo took Poll's gin out of his hand and drank it before chucking the tin cup over the side of the ship.

"Captain, what on earth was that?" Sergeant Peng came over.

"I do not know," said Glabeo, "but one thing is sure, it's dead."

"And so is Hills." Poll laughed, leaning on the rail.

"What do you mean?" asked Sergeant Peng, looking at Poll with a frown.

"Hills was on that beast. He went down with it, with an almighty splash." Poll raised his arms and whooped at the sky.

"Shut up, Poll!" Glabeo scanned the water with his telescope. "Send a lifeboat out there with three men."

Sergeant Peng ran over to the nearest lifeboat, near which he saw four men hanging off the side trying to pull someone up.

"Who's that?" He asked.

"Rusty Miller, sir." The men got Rusty, who was clinging onto the rope net, up to the rail. Rusty looked as white as a ghost, his eyes wide, and was shivering from the cold. Sergeant Peng knelt down and grabbed Rusty by his shoulders and pulled as the others lifted him up by his legs to lay him down on the wooden deck.

"Take this man down to sick bay," Sergeant Peng ordered. "Plus I need two men to come with me." He stood up, looking down at Rusty. "Right, who is with me then?" asked Sergeant Peng as he leapt onto the side of the ship, holding onto the rigging.

"Well, who's coming with me?"

All the crew looked up at Sergeant Peng in silence, with only the sound of the sea, the wind, and the creaking of the ship.

"I see – no volunteers …" he said as he walked along the edge. "Then I'm going to have to pick two of you myself. Right, you there." He pointed his finger at a man in a red coat who was scratching his bald head.

"What, me?"

"Yes, you and the guy next to you. What's your name?"

"Oh, my name is Jack Nickels and this is Eddy Mouthing." Jack indicated the fat man with a ring in his lip, chewing on tobacco.

"Yes, let's do this," said Sergeant Peng as he jumped off the side.

The crew lowered one of the little lifeboats into the dark sea. Sergeant Peng sat at the bow, and Jack and Eddy at the stern, with their oars dipping swiftly into the water. Sergeant Peng looked out with his telescope.

"Hills, are you there?" he shouted, looking to the left and then to the right. "Hills, are you there?" he shouted again.

"Hey, do you really think the boy is still alive?" Eddy whispered to Jack.

"No, no one can survive in this cold for so long. This is just a waste of time," he replied, not noticing that Sergeant Peng was looking straight at him.

"If you two think this is a waste of time…! I will not have that talk on this boat." Peng went back to looking through his telescope. The little boat went round and round for hours as the air got colder and colder. Eddy's hand had turned pale and numb as he kept rowing and rowing.

"This is useless. All we're doing is going round and round."

"Shut up, Jack!" Sergeant Peng shone the lantern closer to the water. "Stop… Jack, look here!" Sergeant Peng leaned over the side. "Hold the lantern."

"Yes, sir."

Under the deep water, blowing little bubbles from a cave, watching the small rowboat with big white eyes, lurked something that glowed bright red and yellow. As the boat moved, the creature moved, swimming along the coral reefs, changing its colours to blend into the surroundings, scaring the little fishes as it went.

Jack shone the lantern into the water for Sergeant Peng. "There's something down there," Peng said.

"What?" Jack just sat there hanging the lantern over the edge.

"Look there! Did you see that? Something red and yellow?"

"No."

"Jack, you're not even looking." Sergeant Peng pulled Jack over to look at the water. "Can you see it now?" With that, Sergeant Peng pushed Jack's head into the water and then pulled him back.

"Are you trying to kill me?"

"Well, you looked like you needed to wake up."

"This is rubbish. Kimy Hills is dead!"

"Jack, if you say that, then Captain Glabeo will blame you. Kimy Hills is the Sails Minister's son. That's why we must find him, even if it's only his body."

"Great, that's just great." Jack slumped back into his seat wiping the water from his face. "The quicker we find him, the better."

Sergeant Peng went back to looking.

As the *Royal Westneck* rocked gently in the water, Captain Glabeo visited the sick bay where Rusty was lying in bed still looking as white as a ghost. Captain Glabeo sat down at the end. "Miller, how are you doing?"

"I'm … sir, I'm … sir." Rusty tried to answer him.

"I know, I know. I saw you and Hills making friends up there in the lookout before that beast broke the masts. We've sent a search party to look for Hills, it's been hours, I'm afraid he won't survive these icy waters. I'm sorry, Miller, I'm afraid I'm going to have to call off the search."

Rusty looked at him with tearful eyes and tried to lift his arm. "Get some rest, Miller," said Captain Glabeo as he walked off.

The ice-cold wind blew over the waters, but the light of the lantern burned bright as the rowboat went round and round, Sergeant Peng periodically shouting with a now scratchy voice.

"Sir, I think we should turn back!" shouted Eddy as his hands started turning blue. Ice had formed around his nose.

"Just one more time, Eddy."

"Sergeant, admit it. Hills is gone!"

But Sergeant Peng looked out over the water hoping that Kimy would appear somehow. Still nothing came up out of the deep, and Peng sat back down, watching Jack and Eddy shiver.

"Sir, I know you would like to find Hills, but we are going to freeze to death if we don't get back to the ship."

Still Peng said nothing and then a loud horn blew from the *Royal Westneck.*

"Sir, they're telling us to go back."

"I suppose we should… turn the boat." Peng gazed at the water.

The creature glowed as it followed the rowboat back to the *Royal Westneck,* swimming around rocks and little caves and through a sunken wreck. Its tail brightened as it moved swiftly down through a canyon and then to a cave in the canyon wall. It came to rest and watched the *Royal Westneck* above intently.

"Well, Sergeant, what am I going to tell his father?" Captain Glabeo greeted Peng, who was climbing up the net to the deck.

"Captain, I don't think that Hills is dead. He's still out there – I can feel it." Peng looked back out over the sea, clenching his fist tight.

"Hills is dead." Captain Glabeo patted Peng on the back. "No one can survive out there. I'm sure he is in a better place. Now we have got to get our masts fixed before we can do anything."

"Yes, sir," replied Peng, "but I will need you to send a message to the capital and tell them our position."

"Okay, but what will I say about Hills, sir?"

"Nothing yet, Sergeant. Nothing yet."

Glabeo walked off, leaving Peng on his own under the moon, looking out across the ocean. "Hills, I hope you are okay."

CHAPTER SIX

Fire of Wrecks

It took a few days for the crew to repair the masts. Once they were moving again, every ship the *Royal Westneck* passed was on fire. It sailed between them, passing through black smoke, hot ash and bright explosions as the boats around them burnt and sank. The heat of the air was stifling, and sparks singed holes in the sails of the *Royal Westneck*. The crew covered their faces to avoid getting burnt. Some of them dumped buckets of water over their heads to keep cool. Captain Glabeo stood at the top of the deck holding a handkerchief over his mouth and nose. "Hold on, hold on!" he shouted, pointing at the man at the wheel, who was sweating.

"The ship won't hold! The ship won't hold, sir!" shouted Jack as the rope of one of the sails burnt through. The huge sail crashed down towards him. Sergeant Peng tried to reach for him as the sail smashed into his back, sending Jack flying into the window of the Captain's cabin. The sail bounced back the other way, knocking more crew off the side of the ship as they yelled and plunged into the water. Sergeant Peng ran and jumped through the window before the sail collided into the wooden frame which splintered around him as he landed near Jack.

"Jack are you okay?" There was no answer. "Jack?" Sergeant Peng nudged him. "Jack, come on." A slight groan came from him. Sergeant Peng turned Jack onto his back, but when he saw his face he sat back in horror. "Oh my…." the left side of his face was bloody with little bits of glass stuck into his flesh. "Help! Someone!" Sergeant Peng shifted to be closer. "I'm here," he said, ripping his sleeve off and holding it up to Jack's bleeding face.

"Grab the sail!" shouted Captain Glabeo as he climbed down the ladder. Some of the crew ran after the bit of rope that was hanging from the sail as it went backwards and forwards. "I've got it!" one man shouted, his hand reaching higher than the rest, but the rope quickly flung past him, rapping his hand and giving him a burn mark across his palm for his trouble.

"I've got it!" shouted another as he was dragged around by the sail. "Help me!" he cried as he collided into a barrel. Four men ran to grab him as the rope lifted him into the air.

"Come on!" shouted Captain Glabeo. "Stop messing around and grab the damn thing!"

"Sir, you should see this." Eddy gave him the telescope.

"What?"

"I think there's someone on that burning wreck, sir." He pointed, and Captain Glabeo raised his telescope to his eye.

"What? It can't be Kimy Hills … My word. Go and tell Sergeant Peng, we need a rescue team."

Kimy waved at the *Royal Westneck*, he was drenched, his white shirt severely ripped. He rushed to the stern as water rose up the deck.

"Where is he?" Sergeant Peng rushed to Glabeo's side.

"He's over there on that burning wreck, its sinking fast. Get on the boat and get him, Sergeant!"

The men worked quickly to lower one of the boats, but they heard a loud twang as one of the ropes got unhitched.

"What is it? Get it down!" shouted Captain Glabeo.

"We can't – it's jammed," replied a small man known as Hamster.

"For goodness sake, cut the rope, Hamster!" Glabeo pulled out his sword, lifted it high, and swung it down to chop the rope in half. The little boat fell and splashed into the water. "That's how we do it." Glabeo grinned at Hamster. "Take him with you, Sergeant," he said pointing at Eddy.

The burning wreck was falling apart. One of the tall ship's mast's had collapsed and fallen into the water, Kimy watched the floating pieces. He looked up and spotted their rowboat.

"Keep rowing, keep rowing!" shouted Sergeant Peng.

Kimy looked down at his legs, which were tied together by a rope, it hung off the edge into the water, bubbles rising around it.

"Kimy, Kimy are you OK?" shouted Sergeant Peng as they approached the burning wreck, but Kimy was too scared to shout, instead he waved them off frantically.

"Sir, I think he wants us to go back," said Eddy.

Sergeant Peng picked up some rope from beside him, but Kimy started frantically waving even more, moving up and down as much as he could.

"Sir, something doesn't feel right about this."

"Well, it looks okay from here, Eddy."

"Something seems fishy, sir. How can Kimy be here when we left him for dead after hours of searching? Even a great swimmer couldn't survive in these cold conditions."

"Well, I'm not leaving him out here."

"But, sir, what if it's some sort of ambush?"

"If it's an ambush, then so be it."

"What's taking them so long?" Glabeo looked through his telescope as Poll came up to him, swaying as he walked, clearly drunk.

"Still no Hills, ah diddum's, well…" Poll burped loudly. Glabeo turned to look at him.

"For your information, Kimy Hills is over there."

Poll took a gulp of beer, some gushing out of his mouth and onto his clothes. "Kimy Hills is dead and his captaincy is no more." He staggered around until Glabeo grabbed him by the scruff of his neck and pushed him back against the recently repaired mast. "You're just a drunk that picks on people like Hills because his father is a Sails Minister. Aren't I right, Poll?"

"No, it's because his father took away my captaincy of my lovely *Whitejack*, because he thinks I led them into enemy territory."

Glabeo threw him onto the deck. "So it was you in command at Cans." He drew his sword and lightly pierced the skin of Poll's neck. "You made us lose a lot of good men that day." Glabeo's face looked like he was going to explode. "You and your so-called comrade, Lip May."

"Lip May is a good friend of mine." Poll's face started to sweat.

"Oh really?" Glabeo leaned in close. "Yet we never met him, did we?" Poll crawled slowly away. "You let us chase that ship from Mallet so we would enter a trap." The captain placed his boot on Poll. "And I suppose you knew that, didn't you?"

"I was only following orders!" shouted Poll.

"I'll see to you after we've got Hills back!"

Kimy waved and waved desperately at the small boat. But Sergeant Peng was undeterred and threw his rope over the railing of the burning wreck. Kimy looked over the side to where his rope went under the water, bigger bubbles started emerging. He watched Sergeant Peng, trying to climb aboard.

"I don't like this, sir," Eddy said looking at the ropes tied around Kimy's legs.

"Come on, get up." Sergeant Peng pushed Eddy over and then, with a big jump, he boarded the wreck himself. Kimy turned white, he noticed from the corner of his eye that the bubbles around his rope were getting bigger and rising more frequently.

"Hills, we're coming!" Sergeant Peng started carefully making his way to where Kimy was. The ship began to rock and then started to shudder. Sergeant Peng and Eddy stopped walking and clung to the railing as another mast full of fire and smoke came crashing to the deck.

"Turn starboard!" shouted Captain Glabeo as he looked on from the *Royal Westneck*, concerned about the smoke that he saw shooting straight up into the dark sky.

Kimy lay on the deck, covered in ash. As he pulled himself up by the railings, he sneezed. Kimy looked down to where Sergeant Peng had been, but all he could see were pieces of burning mast crackling in the fire. "Sergeant Peng? Sergeant Peng?" Kimy shouted as he walked along the top deck, finally finding the courage to speak. Kimy paused at the stairway, with the rope around his leg tightening as he moved, but then the rumble of a cannon fire came from nowhere. Kimy looked out to sea and saw the *Royal Westneck* firing. He tried to see what they were shooting at and then realised the noise was coming from the front of his burning wreck. Cannonballs whistled as they zoomed through the air, splashing sea water over the front of the fiery ship.

The wreck trembled for a minute with Kimy leaning on the railing, his hands clenched around a wooden beam. Then the shuddering stopped. "Sergeant Peng?" yelled Kimy.

"Stay ready," shouted Captain Glabeo as he peered through his telescope.

Black mist started blowing up from the hollow and flowing over the deck. Kimy knelt down as he saw it gently moving towards him. He tucked his head down towards his chest, looking at the floor and briefly shut his eyes as he felt hot ash hit his back. Next his face started burning in agony. Kimy fell onto the deck and tried to crawl to where his rope went over the railing, but as he moved he found it difficult to breathe. His vision went blurry. Kimy reached out his hand to where the rope went over. Suddenly little round lights emerged from the mist. Kimy watched them rise up out of the sea. The lights came to a shimmering stop with a loud horn noise that made it hard for Kimy to hear; then hundreds of shadows leapt out of the mist. They jumped high and landed onto the deck of the burning wreck.

Kimy tried to keep his eyes open but kept failing, he watched one of the shadows leap over to him. Kimy fell asleep, his head smacking against the wooden deck. "Kimy … Kimy …" said a voice in Kimy's ear, he felt a poke to his right shoulder.

"Get away!" Kimy shouted, as he thought he woke up.

"It's all right. Calm down, my boy."

"D-Dad, what am I doing here?" Kimy looked around the kitchen.

"Son, you are neither here nor there." Foofur grinned at him. Kimy saw his mum standing on the porch, watering her lemon tree, singing at the top of her lungs. "What's going on?" Kimy panicked in confusion as he got up from the chair.

"*The Land of Cass is up the flass, Kimy. The Land of Cass is up the flass,*" said Foofur as James, Rosetta, and Puss walked up to him slowly and started repeating Foofur's words.

Kimy walked backwards, petrified, he wondered what was going on as he reached the corner of the room. They repeated the words louder and louder as they came closer and closer, their mouths grinning. Their fingers turned into claws as they approached. "Dad, Mum, James, Puss?" shouted Kimy, looking at each of their faces as he spoke. But they just kept on coming. Kimy pushed himself deeper into the corner, his eyes staring at his dad's claws as they touched his chest. "Help!" yelled Kimy.

"Kimy … Kimy … Kimy!" said a voice in his left ear, shaking his shoulders.

Chapter Seven

The Crew of Slime

Kimy gradually opened his eyes and saw a blurry outline standing in front of him. "Kimy, it's me, Sergeant Peng." Kimy sat up and found himself on a hefty, rusting, metal bed. He rubbed his eyes.

"Sergeant Peng, what's going on?"

"We're trapped, Kimy. Whatever those shadows in the mist were, they've captured us. There's no way out." Sergeant Peng walked over to a small round window, dragging a heavy black ball chained to his left leg. "I've got no idea what we're in, but we're under the water." Sergeant Peng peered out the window, as though to confirm that the impossible was still true.

"I don't know what happened," Kimy said, rubbing his head. "All I saw was this shadow jumping up, coming at me, and that was it."

"Hmm, something was in that mist all right." Sergeant Peng leaned on the window, tapping his chin with his finger. "Kimy," he asked as he turned around, "do you recognise this place?"

"I do." Kimy sighed while looking around. "I was in here. These people are not at all like us. Their skin is green and shiny with mucus all over them. They used me for bait." Kimy looked down at the floor. "I think they wanted to bring down the *Royal Westneck*."

"Do you know why they're doing this?" Sergeant Peng took a seat on the other bed.

"No, they talk in a different language. I don't understand them."

"Great. That's just great."

"Where's Eddy?" Kimy asked.

"I don't know. I hope he got away. Kimy, is this how you survived – in this vessel that swims under water?"

"Yes, sir. I thought I would never see you again – we travelled under the water going deeper and deeper, I had to eat weird things to survive, like green snot that makes you heave." Kimy glanced around the dark, damp room they were in. It had a table sat against the wall with two rusty chairs. Termites crawled in and out of the holes they had eaten in the wooden walls.

"This place stinks to high heaven," Sergeant Peng complained. Suddenly a loud bang came from the door and large amounts of water leaked in around it. Kimy and Sergeant Peng froze, their eyes fixed on the door that vibrated each time the thing hit it. Bang, bang, bang. "Rrrrrrrrooooogggg!"

Kimy looked over at Sergeant Peng. "It's food time," he whispered. The thing smashed the door open. Water poured in from the hall, and flashes of lightning bounced in from the corridor.

"Look out!" shouted Sergeant Peng as the lightning bounced around him, burning holes into his coat. The lightning wreaked havoc as it smashed into the walls, making thousands of wooden splinters fly. Kimy and Sergeant Peng quickly got under the beds as whole pieces of the ceiling collapsed, bringing more water with it. Rotten pieces of ceiling smashed down onto the beds and floor.

Kimy yelled.

"Kimy, are you okay?"

"My hand!" shouted Kimy. "My hand is trapped. I can't get it out!" Kimy panicked and grabbed his left arm with his right. Then a deep croak made Kimy and Sergeant Peng both look at the door. Sergeant Peng felt numb, his eyes fastened on the doorway as a great round figure entered.

"Krroogg!" it blurted with its neck streaching out like a balloon. Sergeant Peng kept as quiet as he could, but a buzzing reached his right ear, and something with eight legs landed. He tried hard to ignore the bug's tickly feet, which walked around the top of his ear, not wanting to draw attention to himself.

The figure at the door croaked again as water swept in, but it remained unmoved by the wave. The table and chairs had toppled over, and the breathing space under the bed grew smaller. "Sergeant!" Kimy shouted as another wave splashed him and he accidentally gulped some water.

The water swept everything to the back of the room, slamming Kimy into the corner with the bed flipping and trapping him. Kimy tried to push the bed off, his arms in agony as more and more water pounded the bed, resisting him. Kimy pushed with all his might, his face turning red and his jaw tightening as he tried to summon all of his strength. Flashes of lightning still bounced around the room. The water kept rising, and Kimy was beginning to feel the cold, it drew the heat from his body. He pushed harder, though his arms were in unbearable pain and his legs could no longer feel the weight of the bed. "Sergeant!" Kimy shouted again and again, but there was no answer.

All Kimy heard was the water pouring from the hole in the ceiling that came down like a waterfall.

The figure at the door hopped slowly in as he heard Kimy's shouting. It stopped in the middle of the room, where the water poured through, splashing over its head. Kimy's head was just barely held out of the water.

"Sergeant Peng!" shouted Kimy once more as he choked on water. "Are you there?"

The figure turned quickly and hopped over. Between the pain and the freezing cold water, Kimy's arms finally gave up. He released the bed and raised his arms, unintentionally catching the figure's attention. Quick as anything, a long sticky tongue shot around Kimy's arms, yanking them together. Kimy tried with all his might to unleash his arms by swinging his body, but it was no good, as the water was now up to the level of his mouth.

The bed shuddered as the figure's tongue tried to pull Kimy out. "Aaaarrrr!" yelped Kimy as his legs were forced against the beams that trapped him. Water still poured into the room from the door and ceiling, with lightning crashing from wall to wall. Sergeant Peng finally appeared from under the muddy water, taking a deep breath of air as he cautiously swam around the back of the figure which was so focused on pulling Kimy out.

"What are you?" whispered Sergeant Peng. His back bumped against a floating piece of wood. "It's time to find out." He grabbed the plank and raised it, approaching the creature slowly against the force of the water. Kimy, meanwhile, tried to bite the red tongue as it pulled him tighter and tighter. Sergeant Peng swung the plank and whacked the figure around its chunky head, forcing it to loosen its grip around Kimy's arms and sending it crashing down into the water. "Kimy, are you okay?"

"Yes, just get this bed off me!" cried Kimy in agony.

Peng quickly grabbed the bed. "Right, Hills, on the count of three, push the bed up from underneath. Ready?"

"Yes, ready!"

"One, two, three!" They pushed and pulled, and slowly the bed lifted from Kimy's legs. "Kimy, move out!" Kimy quickly pushed himself right back into the corner as Sergeant Peng couldn't hold the bed anymore.

"Can you feel your legs?"

"No, I can't even move them!"

"This water is making it hard to walk." Sergeant Peng lifted Kimy out of the cold water by his arm. "And the ball chained to my leg is digging into my ankle." he added. Kimy looked at the figure lying face down in the muddy water.

"These creatures remind me of the frogs in my mother's pond."

"I've never seen these things. They must be new to our planet."

"Sergeant, they can't be new: The Gates of Dreams haven't opened yet." Then they heard a deep sucking noise; it seemed to shake the whole vessel.

"What's going on?" demanded the sergeant as the shuddering intensified. Kimy looked out the window and noticed giant tentacles moving up and down.

"This is something else," said Kimy as they both looked out into the dark ocean.

Thousands of underwater vessels lurked around the one Kimy and Sergeant Peng were on. They quickly and quietly swam through the sea with their green-and-black tentacles, heaving themselves along the seabed, shaking the ground as they moved.

"We're going to die, Kimy, if we don't get off this vessel!"

"There's nowhere to go, Sergeant. We could be at the very bottom of the ocean!"

"So, Hills." Sergeant Peng frowned at him. "Would you rather die from getting eaten or risking trying to escape?"

"There is no way we are going to hold our breath for that long. The best idea is to wait until the vessel has surfaced and then try to sneak out. Besides, there are a whole lot of other vessels out there with this one," responded Kimy.

"Okay, Hills, if you think it's a better idea to sit here and wait days, or weeks, trying to survive being tortured…"

"Fine, Sergeant, but you can do it on your own."

"Kimy, you will do as I say. I am your sergeant, and look, no one is guarding the door." The sergeant approached the smashed-up doorway.

"It's all a matter of timing," Kimy argued while the sergeant peeked around the corner. "Timing is the key to survival, and doing it your way, Sergeant, is a death sentence."

"I know my commands, Hills, and you are going to follow them!"

"Sergeant," raged Kimy, "you have no idea how many of these things are out there. You have no idea of the layout of the vessel. You don't even know if the *Royal Westneck* still sails or where it is!"

"I risked my life trying to save yours. I know what I'm doing! Right, I'll be back to get you." He walked quickly out of the room and into the darkness.

"You're going to get us both killed," said Kimy, pulling his sword slightly from its case.

The dark vessel stunk of rotting fish, and previous victims were scattered about its bow. As for the fat jumping creatures, they slurped on fish remains, wrapping their tongues around flesh and ripping chunks off. Most of the ship was full of blood stained water with bones floating in it. Rats crawled down the few dry corridors. Many of the green slimy creatures slept standing up or lying in their own mess, snoring loudly. Sergeant Peng moved swiftly through a corridor up to where he noticed a beam of light through a closed door. Odd noises were coming from it. He put his ear firmly against the door, listening. After some indiscernible sounds, there came a moan that sounded familiar. "Stop, please, stop! I don't understand you," cried a voice.

"Glum rog *glum glum!*"

"Please, *noooo!*"

"That's it," whispered Sergeant Peng as he looked around for something sharp. "I can't take this anymore." He noticed where the galley was and walked slowly towards it, dragging his ball and chain behind him. "There's got to be something I can use to cut this damn thing off." He looked around at the cracked blood stained wooden worktops covered with abandoned rotting carcasses, maggots, and flies. "This place is hell!" Sergeant Peng held his nose as he crossed the galley, opening the cupboard doors as he went.

As the ship moved faster with the fleet, Kimy stared at the doorway, wondering what was best to do. Then he heard someone screaming in the distance. Without thought, he drew his sword and leaned towards the dark hallway anxiously. He heard the sound of a whip slashing. It made Kimy's hairs stand on end. He was facing the smashed doorway, so he didn't notice the creature in the muddy water quietly stand up, it looked at Kimy with its beady eyes and licked its lips with its gigantic tongue as it walked slowly towards him.

Sergeant Peng swiftly explored the galley, lifting rusty pans from the rack. This would be good to knock those green slobs out, he thought.

"Please no more!" shouted the voice from inside the closed room.

Peng came across a large knife behind another wooden cupboard door. He grabbed the rusty handle and started sawing away at the metal chain around his leg. But as he sawed, two green figures came down the corridor towards the room that the racket was coming from. As they walked, their keys jangled. They gave the wooden door a massive smash with their webbed hands while Peng moved out of sight behind one of the wooden worktops.

"Rog rop!" shouted one of them as the other stared into the galley.

"Fhug, mubg," said someone from inside the room.

"Help, please! No, not me!"

As the door burst open, Peng realised why the voice was familiar. "That's Eddy," he whispered just as the chain came off. Sergeant Peng moved quietly and quickly to the entrance, listening to Eddy's cries. "Come on, you beast." He poked his head around the entrance. The screaming now mingled with munching noises. "Come on, I can do this." Sergeant Peng lifted his pan up and commanded himself, "Go!" He rushed into the corridor, but as he came to the open doorway of the room, red liquid splattered down his left side. Sergeant Peng stood still, staring in shock as the blood ran down his face. The noise stopped for a minute as the figures looked at the newcomer in surprise. Peng gripped the pan tighter as he realized in horror that their tongues were wrapped around Eddy. Sergeant Peng lifted the pan quickly and smashed it into the nearest creature's back, making it fly into the wall. The other two leapt high with their tongues snapping out to catch Sergeant Peng. With all his might Peng smashed into them both with the pan, which knocked them into the corridor with an almighty crash.

"Eddy!" Peng rushed over to the body on the floor. "Eddy, come on!" He looked into Eddy's staring eyes and knelt down beside him as tears fell down his cheeks. Eddy's body lay still. The silence felt like a distant anger growing within Sergeant Peng. "Come on, Eddy, let's get you out of here." He lifted Eddy's body over his left shoulder and slowly turned to the door. But as he looked up, a group of the slimy green creatures, with pointed spears quickly blocked the exit. Sergeant Peng just stood there as the figures surrounded him.

"I see …" said a deep voice, and Peng tried to figure out who had spoken. "You think you can escape us?" A green figure in a white-and-black sparkling robe stepped to the fore.

"You can talk?"

"Yes, I can, to learn more about our new prey." Saliva ran down his green chin.

"What are you?" ask Peng.

"We are called the Frogmen of the Enchantment. Why are you coming through our territory?"

"This is not a territory," replied Sergeant Peng.

"You are wrong." The frogman scratched his neck. "You see, the mermaid queen gave this water to us, but when we came here, your ships were passing through. Seeing as you and your comrade are here …" He looked at Eddy's body. "You shall work for me."

"I only work for His Majesty," spat Peng.

The frogman leader hopped around him. "It's either work or be eaten." All of the green frogmen started licking their lips as Kimy was dragged in, his hands tied. "You see, my crew doesn't know what to eat on this planet, but eating your species tastes like," he rubbed his fingers together and kissed them, "chicken, which we like a little."

"So you think you can use us for food!"

"Yes, but instead of eating you, I think we can find some other use for you."

Kimy spoke up then. "I would rather work for you than be eaten. I think it's a good idea." Kimy tried to meet the sergeant's eyes.

"Okay, Hills, if you think it's for the best, I'll stay with you." He reluctantly looked at the frogman.

"Ah, great," he said, hopping about. "As you know your planet so well, we have a job for you, but as for your friend…" He glanced at Kimy. "You cannot use your legs. You might as well be eaten."

"*No!*" shouted Sergeant Peng. "I am not working for you without him."

"Well," said the frogman, "he's no good if he cannot use his legs."

"Truly, he knows more about our planet than I do."

"Okay, then you both will have to navigate and work as part of my crew if you want to live." He took a seat on the chair next to the table. "You will tell us all about Gollo and how to get there," he added, twisting his keys in his webbed hand and smiling grimly at them both.

CHAPTER EIGHT

The Fall of the Valley Inn

The sun was shining high over the hills, the trees plump with sparkling green leaves and red blossom. Horses galloped along a dusty road, pulling a black carriage that swerved and jumped from the frantic pace. The driver held a long whip, slashing at his horses if they slowed. The wheels sent the dry dust flying as the carriage charged towards a town called Finley.

Finley was the centre of construction for many of the king's ships. The tall trees that grew there were strong and made sturdy ships. But Finley was in a sorry state. The people were poor. They'd close their little cottage doors when the debt collectors came. Some homes were burnt to the ground in punishment when the owners couldn't pay. Some lived in hastily built dwellings off the beaten path to escape notice, but it wouldn't be long before the collectors found them and dragged the whole family out to throw them into the jail wagon.

The black carriage stopped at the shipyard, and the workers stared at the covered windows as they walked by.

"We are here, sir." The driver opened the door.

"Thank you," said Foofur as he jumped out, giving the man ten doubloons before walking up to the warehouse door, head held high, listening to the sound of drilling and hammering going on all around. Foofur heard Mr Cake muttering as he stepped inside.

"This is it. Put that there, and this …" Mr Cake lifted a bit of metal, putting his finger on his chin in thought.

"I see," said Foofur. Mr Cake jumped out of his skin, clutching his chest.

"Mr Hills, I see you are here to check up on me."

"Yes, maybe, but mainly I am here to see the plans you have drawn up for this engine ship."

"Ah yes, the plans, of course." He rummaged through his tattered brown shoulder bag as Foofur drew closer. "Aha!" he said as he pulled out a scroll of paper tied with green string. "These are great plans, Mr Hill," he said, wandering over to the tatty table and laying the papers out. "We will build this ship out of aluminium."

Foofur looked anxiously on. "You really think a metal ship will not sink, Mr Cake?"

"Of course not, sir. We have done some tests with metal elements."

"Very well," replied Foofur. "Have you got a copy for the king?"

"A copy is being made at this very moment. How are your family, sir?"

"They are as well as can be expected."

"It is unfortunate that your home came under attack."

"My family are fine. My wife is resting in hospital, and so is my boy's fiancée." Foofur pointed to another set of plans. "What are these?"

"This," Mr Cake hurried to explain, "is the greatest bit of work, something special." He winked.

"Look, Mr Cake, I need these plans pronto," Foofur said as the inventor wandered around muttering to himself, counting on his fingers. "*Mr Cake!*" shouted Foofur.

"The plans are being copied right now and will take a couple of days, sir." Cake wandered out the warehouse door.

"Mr Cake! Mr Cake!" shouted Foofur, raising his arm to try and get his attention. When Foofur rushed out the warehouse door in annoyed pursuit, Mr Cake had vanished. "Damn!" Foofur started scanning the area. "What is wrong with this man?" Foofur walked around the shipyard and watched as wooden ship frames came together. Ropes heaved timber and workmen rolled wheelbarrows up and down the gangway full of shingle and chippings. Strong horses pulled great big blocks of wood up to the fittings. Foofur spotted Mr Cake walking into a tea shop outside the yard. "I see you now, Mr Cake, and you will give me the plans," Foofur muttered as he started walking towards him.

Foofur peered through the window and watched the inventor queue up. Mr Cake muttered to himself as he came up to the counter where the bored man asked lazily, "Yes, what can I get you, sir?" His green apron was covered in food, and his curly beard was so long, it brushed the countertop.

"Oh yes, I will have your finest crab lettuce chunk with a cup of hot soup."

"Yes, coming right up." The man walked into the smoky kitchen while Foofur slowly joined the back of the queue watching Mr Cake select a table, sit down, and slip his right hand into his shoulder bag.

"Ah yes, here it is," Foofur heard Cake murmur as he pulled out his glasses. "Just a little adjustment…" As he started to pull out the plans, another hand beat him to it.

"Look, Mr Cake," said Foofur, "I have not got all day to play games with you."

"What?" Mr Cake looked puzzled. "I am not playing games, sir. I've got work to be getting on with."

Foofur ignored this. "I need to know how long the build is going to take." He took the opposite seat, looking at Mr Cake.

"Do you ever wonder, Mr Hills, whether, even if we build this remarkable ship, this planet will be safe?"

"Time will tell. If this ship does not work, then so be it."

"*Nooo!*" shouted Mr Cake, making Foofur jump. "This ship will be the best, the most amazing ship of all!" He raised his arms and stood up tall, causing everyone to look at him.

Foofur looked dismayed at the inventor's state of mind but tried to appear calm as he said, "So get these plans copied and give them to me."

"They are being printed right this minute, sir, and will take a couple of days." Mr Cake sat down, while the waiter placed his food in front of him.

"I expect these plans to be on my desk in the morning," said Foofur, standing up and walking towards the exit.

The sun had set over the hills of Finley. Foxes rummaged for food, scavenging in the streets and rubbish bins. The golden owl perched on the church's tower, hooted for its mate. All the while a small group of men shiftily clambered out of a rowboat and crept down the back alleys of the town, reaching the old stone bank, which stood tall and mighty from the better economic times of the past. The men surrounded the bank, targeting the long patterned windows. "This is it!" One chuckled as he and another stood at the window.

"Ready, boss?" asked the other, lifting up a barrel of powder, nearly dropping it.

"Stop messing around and get on with it." The men quickly laid a trail of the black powder around all the windows, laughing as they rushed and spilling much of it.

"Come on, let's take cover," shouted the fat one they called their boss. "These people won't know what's hit them."

"Let's do it!" They hid in the bushes on the other side of the road.

"Blow it!" commanded the fat one.

A loud explosion shook the town, and black smoke billowed out. The people of Finley rushed out of their houses, holding candles.

"What's going on?" shouted a tall man in a blue dressing gown. The woman next door pointed down the road.

"There's smoke!" The smoke blew thickly through the streets as people ran from house to house. Foofur came to the window of the Valley Inn, where he was staying, just besides the bank.

"Pirates," he said angrily. He pulled the red curtain open to get a better look, but all he could see was thick smoke.

"Get out, get out!" Someone banged on Foofur's door. "The hotel's on fire!" Foofur quickly picked up his black bag and went out of the room into the smoky corridor, where people were shouting and babies crying. He walked quickly, holding a hanky up to his mouth to breathe through.

"Turn back!" said a man as he rushed up and pulled Foofur to go the other way.

"Hey, calm down, sir!" Foofur shouted, but the man only pulled harder. The hotel's roof started to crumble as flames burst into the hallway, shattering the window as people ran for cover. The stranger pulled Foofur to the end of the corridor.

"It's this one!" He let Foofur go and fumbled for something in his pockets.

"We will suffocate in there, sir." Foofur looked down the corridor, where small flames already licked the walls.

"Where are they?" mumbled the man as his hands moved faster "Where are my keys?" The roof started to collapse, smashing down through each floor as dust billowed into the night sky. Foofur heard the thunderous noise from the floor above.

"Come on, sir!" He pulled the man's waistcoat. Foofur ran back down the corridor watching cracks form along the ceiling, with bits falling away. He forced the last room's door, but as it opened a ball of fire and hot air pushed Foofur backwards and he landed straight on top of the man he was pulling.

"Aaaah, my leg!" he cried but the noise of the fire drowned him out. Foofur lifted his head to look down the corridor as the fire spread along the walls and ceiling, setting the curtain around the window alight.

The ceiling behind them started to collapse. "Come on!" Foofur got up and pulled the stranger to his feet. The hotel shook, Foofur slipped over again, and the floor under their feet cracked down the middle. Foofur quickly found his feet and focused on the burning window. *"Let's go!"* he shouted as he started running, the ceiling and floor falling to pieces behind him. Foofur closed his eyes as he reached the fire, it burned his skin as he ran through it, setting his clothes alight. He leapt through the window just as the walls of the inn came crashing down.

Thick ash spread down the streets and alleys of Finley, covering the place in soot as people ran for cover. The soot cloud encased the roads, coating everything it touched. An alarm sounded at the bank at the same time that the fire wagon burst out of its station, pulled by four horses. The community of Finley stopped and looked at the ruins of the hotel as the dust began to settle. The streets went silent as inhabitants stood in shock, staring at the rubble around them, waiting for someone or something to move.

"Come on, out the way! Let me through!" said someone from the back of the stunned crowd. The crowd moved slowly as a man wearing a top hat and a dark blue overcoat strolled through, holding a lantern high. He turned to the crowd as he came to the front. "People of Finley," he shouted, raising his arms. "Tonight we have come under attack from pirates of the Enchanted Sea. They are too greedy and have robbed us of the treasures we work for day and night." The speaker paused to look at the ruins of the Valley Inn and knelt down, removing his hat. The crowd followed his every move.

"A lot of people will have died in this terrible incident tonight. We must search for survivors that could be trapped in this rubble." He looked at the crowd behind him again. "We, as townspeople, have got to get word to the king. We are poorer than ever now. We need help from outside." He clenched his fist. "It is only a matter of time before we can no longer live here." As he said that, behind him a hand punched up from the rubble. The crowd all shouted as they saw someone struggle up out of the dusty mess. He was covered in white ash from head to toe and could hardly stand. "Help ... Help!" he said pointing back to where he came up from.

"Quick, grab him," shouted a woman in the crowd as they saw him topple backwards.

"Get your shovels and start digging!" shouted the man in the top hat as they rushed up to assist the man in white.

"What's your name?" Some knelt down and lifted him up.

"Fffooof, Foofur," he managed to say, waving his arms. "Go back and get him. Go back and get him."

They lifted Foofur onto a stretcher. "Get who?"

"He's alive. He's alive, trapped down there." Foofur pointed until he was loaded onto the ambulance wagon, crying out in pain and staring at the crackling rubble that was left. The people of Finley worked together to get the wounded out.

"Lie back, sir. Lie back," said a gentle voice.

"Yes, yes." He gazed out the ambulance window.

"You will be all right, sir," said that smooth voice again, Foofur looked up. His eyes widened when he saw the brightest blonde hair shining before him. He noticed the nurse's petite nose as she looked at him, her red lips glistening as she returned to tending his wounds.

The streets were like a war zone with four fire wagons trying to put out the fire at the bank and the inn. "Come on people, this way!" A fireman waved people in the right direction. "Quickly people, this way." The crowd walked slowly in a line, looking up at the inferno.

"Excuse me, sir," said Mr Cake as he walked up to the fireman.

"Keep going, nothing to see."

"Excuse me, sir." Mr Cake pulled the man's shoulder persistently. "What?"

"Is the bank open, sir?"

"Are you insane? The bank is burning! Besides, it's three in the morning." He showed Mr Cake his watch.

"Damn!" he replied, and the fireman stared after Mr Cake as he walked away.

When day broke, the townspeople could see how much damage was done. They walked through the debris filling every street. People were shocked at the absence of buildings in the middle of town. Broken and burnt tables and chairs, and parts of the walls from the Valley Inn laid strewn. Mr Cake walked quietly down the main shopping street, twisting his silver pocket watch as he approached the printing shop. "I suppose Mr Hills will want me to," he muttered as he strolled through the door.

"Yes, sir?" said the man at the counter in a high-pitched voice.

Mr Cake leaned onto the counter. "Yes, I came in here the other day to print some shipping plans," he said, still twirling his pocket watch.

"Oh yes, number twenty-four. Yes, they are ready to be picked up." He reached under the counter and pulled out a white paper package tied with string

"Ah ha, thank you, sir." Mr Cake picked them up quickly and put them into his shoulder bag.

"That will be two doubloons."

Just outside of town and nearly hidden by the green of the forest, the white hospital stood. Outside was the emergency wagon that collected the injured. Foofur was in ward 32, lying peacefully in his bed, Mr Cake poked his head around the corner.

"Mr Hills?" he whispered as he slowly stepped in. "Mr Hills, I have the copy." He put the package on Foofur's table.

"Great," replied Foofur quietly.

"I'm sorry about your hotel, Mr Hills."

"I will give them to the king," said Foofur and Mr Cake walked out, being told by a nurse to let him rest.

Chapter Nine

The Gooroo Lady

The Fleet of Darkness swam deep under the ocean but now caught the glare of the sun as it moved from the Dark Sea waters and neared a small island called Gitaly. "I hope we are near the capital," said the leader of the frogmen as he burst through the door of the lookout tower, where Sergeant Peng was looking through a long telescope. Kimy sat nearby.

"No, Captain, this is not Gollo but another island called Gitaly."

"Ah yes, well we shall stop here anyway, there is someone we know that lives here." He bounced around the viewing area. "You two shall come out with us," he ordered before slamming the door behind him.

"Great," said Kimy, with a sarcastic tone.

"What's wrong? This is our best chance of escape."

"Yes, I suppose so, Sergeant, but my father says that the people who live on Gitaly are cannibals."

"So you mean to say you're more afraid of the Gitaly tribes than these weird frogmen creatures that have just appeared on our planet? Come on, Hills! I want to escape from this hellhole."

The underwater vessels deployed their anchors just off of Gitaly's shores as little boats with smaller tentacles swam from each ship. They swam into a dark cave, where, when they surfaced, they found the walls lit up by candlelight. The little subs heaved their way up to where a cluster of people with flaming torches stood on the cave's beach. Kimy and Sergeant Peng waited to see what the frogmen had brought to their hollow. Wooden houses were fashioned to extend from the cave's walls with wooden ladders running from one to another.

"Where are we going, Captain?" Sergeant Peng asked their captor while he observed the men and women on the beach wearing rags, who stared in turn.

"This is the tribe of the Gooroo," replied the lead frogman.

"The Gooroo?" replied Sergeant Peng

"The Gooroo is a magic woman." Kimy whispered in his ear, "She has voodoo magic."

The Gooroo Lady was full of magic and life. Kimy knew that she was not a myth, as she had lived on planet Galloway longer than most. She was one of the creators of the dream planet. She herself was a strong dream, but, as Kimy knew from the stories his granddad had told him, she had become weak. Another powerful dream came to Galloway and stole her reign from her. She had seemed to vanish from the world. Legend had it that dark figures with red eyes stormed the secret place where she kept the magic element that controlled the dream planet. Most people said she was killed, some said that she'd never even existed.

"Sergeant, as you will see, we have known the Gooroo Lady for some time," said the frogman as he jumped out of the boat and onto the sandy beach. "And, as she found us, she helps us to learn about this planet." He grabbed his spear from the boat.

"You think that her voodoo magic will really help you?" asked Sergeant Peng disgustedly as he too jumped off the boat.

"You are too doubtful, Sergeant. Come with me." They walked through the cave, their footsteps muffled by the sound of running water flowing down the rocky walls and into a stream beside the walkway. "You see, Sergeant, I have a funny suspicion that you want to escape." The leader frogman turned to him as two others stopped nearby, carrying Kimy. "So I think it is best that we chain you up." One frogman swiftly pulled Sergeant Peng's hands together and cuffed them tightly. "This is not the best place to lose you." The leader pulled Sergeant Peng closer and gave him an assessing look. "You want your comrade to walk again? Then move."

Kimy could see that Sergeant Peng was in pain as they walked down tunnels and through streams. Sergeant Peng fell down a couple of times, and one frogman pulled out a long whip and started thrashing him, cutting slits into his Royal Sails coat to keep him moving. They finally came to a wooden door, behind which they could hear shouting and banging.

"Ha ha!" laughed the leader as he turned, rubbing his webbed hands and drooling. Kimy stared at the door as it shook and shook.

"Something is wrong," Kimy said to himself as one of the frogmen walked up. He reached for the black metal knocker and swung it, making it smash into the door loudly. The door made a great thudding noise that shook the entire cave and caused rocks to tumble down the wall. The sounds behind the door stopped. Everything went quiet.

"This is not right, Captain," said Sergeant Peng anxiously.

"Yes, it is right, Sergeant. As right as ever." The frogman leader pointed his spear up high. The sound of loud footsteps approaching echoed from behind the door. Kimy felt like his heart was in his mouth as he stared at the wooden door. A strong wind blew through the passageway, snuffing out candles as it went and then the cave felt silent once again.

"Great!" shouted Sergeant Peng.

"Anything can happen, Sergeant; you just have to wait," said the leader, his tongue licking his lips. Then a great beam of light burst out from the cracks around the door. Kimy lifted his hand to shield his eyes from the unbearable brightness as they all leant slowly forward. The door swung open, banging into the rocky wall. Two large rocky fists came zooming out of the light and then were slowly retracted. As the hands moved, so the light decreased, leaving them in darkness again.

"Is this all a powerful lady has to offer?" asked Sergeant Peng as they approached the entrance again.

"No, Sergeant." The leader lit a torch. "She is only just getting started." He turned to his crew as he reached the threshold. "My fellows!" he shouted. "This is what we have been waiting for – our fortune on this new planet awaits us." He lifted the torch higher, and his crew hopped madly in glee. Suddenly the candleholders on the cave's walls burst into flame, and a thick fog crawled slowly through the cave.

"Who dares to walk in my chamber?" demanded a resounding voice that seemed to come from every direction.

"It is us, oh Gooroo Lady, the Frogmen of the Enchantment. The leader knelt down, his torch still held high. "I have come with a gift." He glanced at Kimy.

"What gift? The only gift I want has been taken from me."

"Yes, but I think these people may be of use to you." Then the cave started to shake fiercely. Entire boulders plunged down from the ceiling. The two frogmen holding Kimy fell backwards, allowing him to slide along the cave's floor. Kimy looked backwards as he slid, noticing a hot bubbling pond that he was heading straight for. Fortunately, Sergeant Peng managed to block him and caught Kimy's eye.

"Hills," he whispered, "these frogmen are up to something." He glanced up at all of them, drooling and licking their lips, some jumping high into the air. The frogman leader got up from the floor and turned to look at his followers again. They fell silent and, like a wave travelling from left to right, started pointing their webbed hands at something behind him. He slowly turned as an individual appeared from out of the mist holding a long wooden stick. The frogman leader took three steps backwards, bowing to her as the thick fists zoomed out again, seemingly from nowhere and pulled off her cloak. Red and white diamonds sparkled down her dress, the top half was predominantly gold and the lower half red. She wore a golden crown with tall white feathers, and her long brown hair hung loose.

"I see, Leader Frogman, that you have brought the whole fleet with you."

"Yes, Gooroo, the whole fleet," he said as she drew nearer to where Kimy was lying.

"So, is this what you call a gift?" She glanced down at him. Kimy looked up at her as he moved a little backwards in fright. "I think that these poor people do not deserve to be my slaves."

The frogman looked annoyed. "Gooroo Lady, these people have been trespassing in my waters."

"The waters are for everyone. You do not control any sea." She walked to her cauldron, which came into view when the mist disappeared.

"But the mermaid queen gave it to me."

"Yes, the sea queen. I haven't seen her in years." She stirred her cauldron. "I know you want to acquire something, and I know that something is power."

"I would like to control the whole planet. You will be queen again, and Galloway will be a better place."

The Gooroo Lady looked at him as he bowed to her again. "I know my reign was taken from me, but that does not mean that you can be king of this planet."

The frogman looked angry at her words. "This planet will be in better hands! All I need to control the magic element is the golden diamond coin that you wear around your neck." He pointed to it.

"Never! Do you think that you will control Galloway through *my* powers just by acquiring the diamond coin?" Her voice was raised, making the cave vibrate again. "There are four things you will need, and they all look different." She stirred the cauldron some more.

The frogman then turned to his people. "I want that necklace, and I will get it!" he shouted.

"Only a person with a true heart and selfless dedication to Galloway can control this planet."

"I have given you all!" The frogman lifted his spear. "I have worshiped the ground you walked on and even provided you with wealth by robbing others. I want to be the most powerful and to have you by my side."

"You have to understand that Galloway chooses its own destiny." The Gooroo Lady raised her arms high, green mist rose from the cauldron in response. Kimy crawled to the cave's wall, looking at the frogman with his crew behind him, holding their spears, ready to pounce.

"There's no going back for you, Gooroo Lady. Just give us the diamond coin and we will be on our way." The other frogmen cheered.

"This diamond coin will always be mine." The Gooroo Lady looked at it. "And will never be yours." The leader's face started turning red as sweat ran down his forehead. He clenched his jaws tight with anger.

"That coin is mine!" he shouted. "Frog tooooggggggg!" He raised his spear, and the other frogmen followed suit.

"Very well!" shouted the Gooroo Lady as she banged her stick on the floor, it shot out a blue beam that surrounded her. The spears were launched, speeding towards her, but they rebounded as they hit the protective blue bubble.

"Aaaaaarrr!" shouted the leader. "Get that coin!" The frogmen charged, bouncing onto the walls and zigzagging unpredictably, shooting out their tongues, trying to catch their prey.

"*En light!*" shouted the Gooroo Lady, pointing her stick at the attacker closest to her. It shot out beams of white light that reflected and struck the frogmen from all directions, brightening the cave. Every frogman that was hit fell to its death. Bodies flew from the impact and smashed onto the rocky floor. Kimy crawled slowly to the corner of the stairs, weaving his way through the frogmen.

"Captain, is this your plan to take over Galloway?" shouted Sergeant Peng, but the leader was too far to hear him. Only those closest could hear over the commotion and turned to glare hungrily. "You green slimy creatures will never take this planet!" Sergeant Peng grabbed a spear from the floor. The frogmen pounced, shooting their tongues out at the same time. Sergeant Peng quickly spun around, extending the spear and cutting their tongues into little pieces. Then he leapt into the air, holding the spear with both cuffed hands above his head. "Yaaaaaarrrrrr!" he yelled at the top of his lungs as he reached the frogmen's height. With all his might, he pushed the spear into the closest one's head, green liquid splattered as the spear went through. Peng quickly pulled it out and rammed it into the next frogman's forehead as he came flying at him. Again he lifted it and stuck it into the neck of another.

Suddenly a rumbling came from the cave, gradually it got louder.

"Sergeant, Sergeant!" shouted Kimy as he threw a spear he found on the floor at a frogman that jumped, shooting his tongue towards him. The spear shot straight through the frogman's chest, turning his face yellow. Kimy moved quickly as the frogman fell and slammed into the floor.

"This is my diamond coin!" The leader and the Gooroo Lady circled the cauldron, the frogman's arms out wide trying to reach her. "You think that you, who holds one of the keys, will stop me from taking it?" demanded the frogman as the Gooroo Lady launched more white beams from her stick.

"There is no way you will take this from me!"

"You are outnumbered." The frogman pointed towards the tunnels. The rumbling got louder and louder, shaking the entire cave as dozens more bouncing frogmen burst in from every entrance to the chamber.

"*Acwer beanen!*" The Gooroo Lady pointed her stick out to the other side of the cave. Lines of green light shot from the end this time, sparking as they zoomed through the air and crashed into the cave walls now caked in dead frogmen. The walls began to move slowly, chunks of rock cracked and formed into thick hands, and then arms and shoulders, which smashed their way out. A gigantic rock foot crashed down onto the cave's floor, treading on frogmen as they tried to scatter. Two massive stone beings moved, slowly, out of the walls.

"This is where it ends." The frogman leader whacked the stick out of the Gooroo Lady's hand and then pushed her down the steps. "You are weak!" He pointed the stick at her.

"Never!" She got up quickly and waved her hand over the cauldron. A thick green mist rose out of it and slammed into the frogman, causing him to fall over and drop the wooden stick, which rolled down the steps of the cave. The stone beings lifted two boulders above their heads.

"*Kimy!*" shouted Sergeant Peng as he fought off three more frogmen, who quickly fell to the floor. "Kimy, where are you?" A great thundering, combined with loud screams, caused Sergeant Peng to turn. He saw the two gigantic boulders rolling quickly towards him, squashing the frogmen that got in the way. "Kimy, where are you?" He turned to run. "Kimy!" The sound of the boulders grew louder behind him. But suddenly, four red sticky tongues wrapped around his arms, pulling him backwards.

"Sergeant!" shouted Kimy as he spotted Peng in the middle of the cave. Kimy tried to stand up, holding onto the rocky wall as he watched Sergeant Peng collapse. Sergeant Peng tried to move, but more and more tongues covered him and started to drag him backwards as he tried to resist, digging in with his feet, scraping the ground as he went.

"Sergeant!" shouted Kimy as he stretched out his hand, trying to get his legs to move. Peng rolled over, holding his wrists, which were still cuffed, up to his face, staring at all the frogmen as they came down on top of him. Kimy watched with helpless tears as more frogmen than he could count piled on top of his commander.

"Sergeant …" Kimy let go of the wall and slid down to the rocky floor, looking at the pile of frogmen as the two boulders smashed down on top of them. "Kimy …" cried out Sergeant Peng as he took one last breath, "… save the coin."

The boulders destroyed more frogmen as they continued through the cave, but Kimy sat there, still holding his arm out, with tears streaming down his face. Coldness fell upon him. He slowly dropped his arm, head down, staring at his legs. Numbness swept over him, but he forced himself to crawl, moving around the mass of dead bodies. There in the middle, lying face up, was the sergeant. Kimy lay next to Peng, in tears. "Please forgive me." After a moment, Kimy sat up, squeezing Peng's cold hand and closing his former commander's eyes. "You can rest now. You are free forever."

A cold silence settled in the chamber as the frogmen lay still and cold. All Kimy could hear was the sound of moving water. The silence was broken as the frogman leader shouted, "Take this!" as he struck the Gooroo Lady with his spear. He watched her clutch her chest and collapse beside her cauldron. "Now, to take one of the four keys."

Kimy noticed her wooden stick, still lying on the bottom step. He started crawling, looking from the stick to the leader, who was still focused on the Gooroo Lady. "You will never take Galloway," she whispered in pain.

"We will see about that." He reached out with his webbed green hands. Kimy crawled faster, over the dead bodies, sliding through the liquid that seeped out of them, until he reached the bottom step.

"At last!" The frogman took hold of the diamond coin that seemed to spark under his red eyes and croaked, "The power of the medallion will be in my hands and will eliminate all enemies! But yes, I need the code to access its power." He looked straight at the Gooroo Lady with a jeering smile. "And I already know it." The Gooroo Lady shook her head as she tried to turn her neck. "*Alfer mayow, sea lio mars.*" The diamond in the middle of the coin started to glow red. "*Af er latam dolight.*"

Kimy quickly reached out his arm and grabbed the stick as beams of red light that came from the coin zoomed around him. Kimy felt fury as he thought of Sergeant Peng. With his eyes blazing, he pointed the stick at the frogman, clenching it tighter and tighter. A massive ball of light burst from it, growing swiftly and lighting up the chamber. The stick started pulsating in Kimy's hand, he had to put both hands around it to hold on. He heard the cries of the remaining frogman growing ever louder, as the light grew brighter until it exploded outwards, throwing

Kimy into the air. He hit the steps hard as he came down. The cave went quiet and dark.

Kimy slowly sat up from the floor, holding his head as blood trickled down his face. The Gooroo Lady pulled herself up, clutching the spear that was protruding from her chest, nearly falling back from the unbearable pain. She looked at Kimy with her big green eyes. Kimy picked up the stick from the floor beside him and looked at its pointy end, running his hand over it as a tear slipped down his cheek. Kimy gazed back at the Gooroo Lady and slowly reached out his hand holding the stick. She snatched it from him and pointed it at him. Kimy's eyes widened with fear as he clenched his arms around his knees. "Please don't kill me!" he cried.

"*Ace humm!*" commanded the Gooroo Lady. A blue ball of light sparkled as it zoomed out of the stick and slammed into Kimy's legs. For a minute Kimy didn't feel anything, but then a great pain seized his feet, making his toes twitch and his leg's shake as the pain climbed. Kimy cried and fell back, staring at the cave's ceiling, gripping the rocks on the cave floor. The pain shot through his legs straight up to his hips. He felt as though his legs were on fire. They glowed bright red. Kimy opened his mouth, his tongue turning a rainbow of colours as his fists cracked the rocks in his hands into dust. His body stretched taut and lifted inches off the floor for a few seconds before resting back down. "My job here is done," said the Gooroo Lady as Kimy stood up slowly, feeling dizzy.

"What do you mean?" he asked, realising that she had fixed his legs and her chest had healed.

"I have found a new protector for this key." She took off the diamond coin and placed it into Kimy's hand.

Kimy looked at the Gooroo Lady in astonishment. "I'm not good enough to become a protector."

The Gooroo Lady smiled. "You will find your path, Kimy." She indicated that he should look into the cauldron. "Your inner spirit is powerful, it takes the form of a small yellow dog," she whispered as she moved her hand over the cauldron. An image of a yellow dog appeared above it in smoke.

"How can a small dog be powerful?" Kimy watched the dog drift up and around the cave's walls.

"Because, Kimy, it is not just a dog, it represents the part of you that keeps you strong, inside." She placed her hand on his stomach, a warm feeling filled Kimy's belly as he closed his eyes. "Kimy, Sergeant Peng is looking down at you from a peaceful and beautiful place. He has done his part on this planet, but for you…" She took her hand away. "You will find that your story has already been written…" The rocks behind her opened like a door, as a glimpse of shining gold sparkled from behind it. "…And it starts right *now*!" So saying, she banged the stick on the floor. Kimy felt wind blowing over him and heard the sound of the sea as salty spray hit his face.

CHAPTER TEN

Kimy Comes Home

Kimy slowly opened his eyes and saw waves hitting the ship he was standing on. "Ah, blue skies." Kimy sighed with relief as the sun hit his face.

"Hills! Where did you come from?" shouted a voice behind him.

"I have no idea, Captain." Kimy turned and looked at Glabeo.

"Thank goodness, at last you are here. Hills, your father would have killed me!"

"Captain!" shouted a crew member. "Captain, there's gold in our hold!"

"Gold? But how?" Glabeo rushed below deck.

Kimy looked out over the ocean and smiled. "Thank you, Sergeant," he said as he waved his hand up high.

The *Royal Westneck* came into port surrounded by small boats carefully sailing around it, hooting their horns. The men of the *Royal Westneck* climbed the rigging once more to adjust the sails and weigh anchor.

"Hills, while you were gone," said Glabeo, walking with him into sick bay, "there were some changes. Poll… we made him walk the plank and marooned him on a deserted island, and Miller, well, you can see for yourself."

Kimy walked up to where Rusty was lying. "Kim," croaked a tired voice.

"Rusty, get some rest." Kimy sat down on the edge of his bed.

"I'm sick and tired of people telling me to sleep." Kimy smiled at that. "Hey."

"What?"

"What is that around your neck?" Rusty pointed to the diamond coin that shone brightly.

"Oh that." Kimy hesitated. "It's something special, from someone."

"Yeah, yeah." Rusty chuckled, sitting up in bed.

"So, how has the ship been?"

"Kim, since you and Sergeant Peng vanished, Glabeo has been on the lookout for you. And he will lose his captaincy when we report in, for not following orders to return immediately."

Kimy felt bad. "Why didn't he leave me and the sergeant?"

"Because Sergeant Peng is Glabeo's best friend."

Kimy stood tall, bracing himself. "I have some bad news, Rusty. Sergeant Peng died trying to save me." Then Kimy rushed out, walking up to the captain's quarters, wiping tears from his eyes. Kimy burst through the door and stood at Glabeo's desk.

Glabeo jumped. "What's the matter, Hills?"

"Sir, I have something I've been meaning to say."

"Look," interrupted Glabeo while tidying his things. "The committee will want to hear the truth about the ship you were on, Hills, and I have been demoted to lieutenant, so I will leave my post on the *Royal Westneck*."

"Sir, I have to say this to you. It's about Sergeant Peng."

Glabeo pulled more things from his drawers, "Hills, its best not to say." Although he was still bent over his drawer, his eyes met Kimy's before he straightened and slammed the drawer shut.

Night fell over the port city, with street lamps and lit windows shining down every lane. Kimy walked slowly from the waterfront. He watched kids run around in the street, their mums shouting from the top windows that they had to come in. Kimy walked all the way to the city square, where he stopped and looked up at the statue in the middle of the park. There he stood, riding his horse with his spear out in front and a big hat covering his face as he leaned into the attack. "So," said Kimy as he observed the diamond coin around the horseman's neck. "I have to hide this." He looked at the real thing around his own. "And keep it safe." Kimy looked up again at the stone rider. "Sir Gollo, how am I going to protect this key to the magic element?"

"Hey! Hey!" shouted a voice behind him. "You're—" Kimy turned around. "You're alive!" His brother wrapped his arms around him, squeezing him tight. "Thank you!" James cried as he looked up at the sky.

"James, my oldest worry-wart brother." They both looked at one another.

"Kim, it is so good to hear your voice." They started walking down the path to where a horse and carriage stood waiting. "Kimy, I hope you have some stories to tell!"

"Well, yes, James – a story of a lifetime."

James put his arm around Kimy. "Well, things have changed here, Kim. Mum and Dad are living in a different cottage at the moment, as the family home has been demolished."

"What?" Kimy stopped in his tracks. "How?"

"Ah, Kim, I will tell you on the way." James opened the carriage door for Kimmy to get in.

The carriage trotted along and Kimy looked out of the window, he watched the night go by, savouring the sight of the north moon. "Kimy?" James looked at him, moving gently with the bouncing carriage. "I thought you would never return home. I thought you were dead." Kimy saw a tear fall from James's eye.

"James, I thought I would never see you or Mum and Dad, and even Granddad, ever again!" The two embraced, grateful beyond words to be reunited. The carriage came to a stop just outside a white house with black beams and a thatched roof. Kimy stepped out of the carriage, as the driver opened the door.

"Home sweet home, eh, Kim?" James put his arm around Kimy's neck,

"Yeah, James, if you can call this home."

"Here are your bags." The driver pulled them from the top of the carriage. Kimy felt warm and happy for the first time, thinking of what his mother might be cooking. He couldn't wait to see the smile on her face.

As Kimy and James walked up to the door, it burst open. "Kimy!" cried his mother, Rosetta rushed up to him, wearing a sling around her right arm. She wrapped her good arm around him, squeezing him tight and kissing him a thousand times on his cheek. "At last you are home!" Kimy then looked up and saw his father standing in the doorway, his arms crossed. A tense silence fell as Rosetta took her hand away and looked up at Foofur. Foofur looked straight at his son, a dark look in his eyes, and then moved aside to let Kimy walk in. Kimy could feel his father's gaze as he entered. Foofur slammed the door, making Kimy stop and close his eyes as his nervousness increased. Suddenly he was pulled into a bear hug in his father's arms.

"Kimy, I'm so glad to see you!"

"So am I, Father." Foofur quickly stepped back and walked off into the lounge as Kimy watched, puzzled.

That night Rosetta cooked Kimy's favourite meal, which was a treat to most of the family. "So," said Kimy, "how was your wedding?"

"Well, Kim…" replied James as Puss put her hand on top of his. "Our wedding plans were on hold until we found you." James swallowed another bite.

"Kimy, I see you have something around your neck," said Foofur peering to get a better look. "Like a coin with a gem in the middle?" Everyone looked at Kimy.

"Well, my adventures are far from over, but this…" Kimy undid some buttons of his clean shirt to better show the coin. "This is something that I didn't want to keep, but its former protector has forced it on me." His whole family stared at the coin.

"How can you bring that into our home?" demanded Foofur, recognising the diamond coin. "That thing will bring bad things to our land."

"What?" shouted Rosetta. "Come on, Foofur, it is just a coin. What would people want with it except to sell it?" She frowned at him.

"That coin holds a power so great…" Foofur looked straight at Kimy. "That is one of the holy keys of the magic element, and it *must* be hidden." Kimy felt the tension increase as everyone looked on in shock. "Where did you get this from?"

"You wouldn't believe me if I told you." He fiddled with his fork nervously.

"Well, if you are the protector, then we must find a place to hide it." Foofur got up from the table, dabbing his mouth with his handkerchief, and walked out of the room.

That night Kimy lay in bed thinking of what to do with the coin.

"Psst," whispered James as he crept into Kimy's room. "Kim, what I was thinking is that you should take that to Granddad." He sat on the end of the bed.

Kimy glanced at him. "Oh, I don't know, James." Kimy set the coin down on to the bedside table. "Maybe I should give it to the committee tomorrow."

"Kimy, I wouldn't give it to them." James stood up and went over to the door. "I think it is best in our granddad's hands, remember all those stories he told us of his encounters with the Gooroo Lady."

As the sun came up, Kimy walked through the doors of the Council Hall, wearing his finest uniform that was dark blue and gold. "Kimy Hills, please come to the stand," the committee spokesperson said as they all checked their big black books. Kimy slowly walked to the seat in the middle of the room. "Kimy Hills, you are aware of the disappearance of the ship the *Fortune*, which you were on? It has been brought to our attention that you were involved in killing your fellow crew members, who were in training as sails men." Shocked, Kimy could feel that he was going to go down for murder as he looked up at King John, who stared at him. The room fell silent until a loan voice shouted behind him.

"Sir! This boy saved a lot of lives on my ship!" Glabeo walked up to where Kimy was sitting. "And he has found the gold from the Golden Fleet. Also, I don't think he would have the nerve to kill his own men, I have only seen him save the lives of others." The king looked on as

Glabeo continued. "My ship would have been pulled under by a beast that was too strong, but Kimy nearly sacrificed his own life to save it."

"Yes, Lieutenant," said the king as he examined his book. "I would like to hear what the boy has to say now." All eyes turned to Kimy.

"Well," said Kimy, "I don't know what happened to the ship, but for the crew that were with me in that rowboat, I did not kill them." Kimy looked at all of them for a moment. "I know there is something wrong with our planet. Things just pop out from anywhere, weird creatures. When I was on Captain, er, Lieutenant Glabeo's ship, we encountered something enormous that nearly sank us, but then I faced something else." Kimy looked directly at the king. "These new creatures were green and slimy, with strong, sticky tongues that extended really far, they called themselves the Frogmen of the Enchantment. They wanted something powerful to control our planet with; plus, they killed and ate men from our crew. We did everything we could to get away, and I lived because of the bravery of Sergeant Peng." Kimy held his hat to his chest. "You can convict me, but it would be for doing nothing to the people I was with that night they disappeared. It is up to you, Your Majesty." Kimy bowed as best he could from his seat.

The room was silent again, waiting for the king's verdict. "Well," said the king, his eyes on Kimy, "I do not know if you did kill those people, but I do know that strange things are happening." He slammed shut his book. "I'm not going to convict Mr Hills, and I'm going to drop all charges." Kimy didn't know what to say. He felt he would fall right out of his chair with relief, but he forced himself to stand and bow before awaiting his dismissal.

"Well done, Kimy," shouted James as Kimy walked into the lobby. "Now let's go and celebrate." He threw his arm around Kimy's shoulders and grinned.

"Hills!" shouted a voice behind them as Major Waddle quickly joined them. "Can I see you in my office?" He pulled out his keys, hardly waiting for an answer.

"Come on, Major, can we do this some other time?" James pleaded.

"No," was the blunt reply. "This is important." He opened the green door of his office.

"Well, Kim, I will see you outside," said James.

Major Waddle's seat creaked each time he moved. He slapped down some papers on his desk and put on his wonky glasses. "Kimy Hills." Kimy stood to attention. "The King and I have been talking." He leaned over his desk to grab his writing feather. "And from what people have been saying, you are one of our finest sailors."

"I wouldn't say I was the finest, sir."

"Yes, well, Lieutenant Glabeo has written to me to say that you should become a captain before you graduate from sail school." Major Waddle stood up and brought out a badge from a cabinet. "I'm now making you Captain Hills." He pinned the badge to Kimy's coat and then saluted him, with Kimy saluting back by instinct more than understanding. Major Waddle resumed his seat and started writing.

"Will that be all, Major?"

"No, Captain Hills, we have decided to put you in command of our newest ship, which is no ordinary ship. She's called the *Royal Aniker* and will be on a special mission." He handed Kimy the papers he had just been signing. "Now, Captain, please have a seat. What really happened out there?"

Kimy sat down. "I don't know where to start…"

"From the top." Major Waddle sat back, giving Kimy his full attention.

"Well, Major," said Kimy, leaning forward to begin his tale. "This is only the beginning."

About the Author

Author M. E. L. Busst was born in England in 1987, in a town called Abingdon, which is situated near Oxford. He moved to Poole in Dorset at the age of twelve and has lived there ever since. His flair for writing stories was acknowledged at the age of six when he entered a story-writing competition at his school and won first prize. He went on to write an entire series of stories as a child, which he constructed into books and hand illustrated. He would read them to lodgers or exchange students from overseas who stayed in the family home. The originals he has to this day.

Busst always struggled in school and was a quiet and shy boy. He found it hard to mix with other children. In 2011, he was diagnosed with high-functioning autism, and, although this finally helped to explain some of the challenges he faced in life, it hasn't kept him from writing exciting stories.

M. E. L. Busst's inspiration comes from his countless walks in the woodland and on the beaches of Dorset with his beloved dog, Oscar. The natural beauty and tranquillity allows his imagination to run wild. This is the first of his books to be published, with more on the way.

Lightning Source UK Ltd.
Milton Keynes UK
UKOW04f2339070115

244122UK00002B/107/P